"You're just a baby," Sholto said harshly

Then very abruptly he pulled the sheet over her. Roslynn clutched at his wrist compulsively. "I've made you very angry."

"Yes, I think you have," he answered dispassionately.

"Then you'll want to send me away."

"The sooner the better."

"I won't go." Half senseless with excitement, she jumped off the bed at him, subsiding against his hard torso. In moments, she had become his creation, not a girl he had taken in but a part of him.

"I can't bear to go," Roslynn wept. "I know I'm pitiful, but I seem to be beyond caring. I love you," she said brokenly.

"It's not love," Sholto told her tenderly. "You're infatuated — but it's only a crush."

The Silver Veil

Margaret Way

Harlequin Books

TORONTO • NEW YORK • LOS ANGELES • LONDON
AMSTERDAM • PARIS • SYDNEY • HAMBURG
STOCKHOLM • ATHENS • TOKYO • MILAN

Original hardcover edition published in 1982
by Mills & Boon Limited

ISBN 0-373-02539-4

Harlequin Romance first edition April 1983

CHAPTER ONE

SHE opened her eyes to a brightly lit room. A man was bending over her. He had remarkable eyes, brilliant, intelligent, so much power. It was that, the power, that fully brought her to her senses.

'How are you?' His voice was quiet but with an underlying vibrant edge.

'Oh——' She stared back at him waxen and dazed, too stunned to think of any more. He had her hand now, using her pulse as an interpreter, and this time she tried to answer his extraordinary authority. Her lips parted and pain moved across her brow as if her very breath hurt her.

'I'm . . . injured,' she faltered.

'Yes.' His eyes were the most elusive colour, neither blue nor green but like the shallows of the sea. 'Tell me your name?'

'Name?' she repeated it after him like an anxious child.

'*Marianne?*'

She winced visibly and tried to shake her head. Her name wasn't Marianne. Marianne was a black void.

'Don't worry,' he said calmly. 'It's quite a fall you had.'

'Who are you?' she asked fearfully, the pain in her head keeping her perfectly still.

5

'McNaughton. Sholto McNaughton,' he answered immediately, the authority of his tone carrying to her distressed mind. 'I'm a doctor.' He bent over her again, staring down into the pupils of her eyes through some instrument. 'Look straight up at me, Marianne.' It was definitely an order and she instinctively obeyed.

After a moment he drew away and she released a long, gasping breath. 'What's happened to me?'

'You were involved in a street accident. You have no recollection of the incident?'

'No, I'm sorry.'

'It will all come back to you,' he said soothingly. 'You know you've been brought into hospital?'

'*Have* I?' Of course she had. Looking beyond him with difficulty she saw another man in the white coat of a doctor, a nursing Sister with a stiff white veil on her head. The Sister smiled at her, softening the professional scrutiny.

'Why, what happened?' She became visibly excited.

'Be quiet now.' He placed a restraining hand on her and there had to be a power in him for her slight girl's body instantly relaxed. 'Tom?' he turned his dark head away to speak to the other man and immediately the girl on the table cried out: 'Don't go away! Promise me you won't go away. I'm sorry, but I don't want you to leave.'

It was an outburst almost hysterical in quality and it cost her dearly, for the waxen skin went grey.

'Hush now, hush!' He caught one of her hands between his own, perturbed by her condition. 'I won't leave you, I promise, but you must stay calm and obey me.'

'I'm sorry.' In her pain and fear she felt excessively dependant and vulnerable. 'I'm *so* sorry.'

'Lie quietly.' His brows knitted and the handsome, austere face looked formidable.

'Yes.' She shut her eyes, comforted by the constant murmur of his voice. He was speaking to the other man, the other doctor, and the Sister was joining in with a few words, but it didn't seem to matter. She could sleep now, repair her tired brain and her body. He had promised her he wouldn't leave her and it seemed vitally important.

'My head aches!' she announced suddenly with a clarity at odds with her previous bewildered little efforts.

'I'll give you something for it.'

She heard his voice again and opened her eyes wide, searching for that brilliant glance. It was obvious she was deeply distressed, but there was trust and an odd dependence in her smoke-coloured eyes. As she had lain unconscious, isolated in her silent world, it had been easy to see the fine, delicate bone structure. Now the small triangle of her face was a mask of suffering and the rose-bronze of her hair damp with sweat.

'Thank you,' she said like a very polite child, and turned greyer than ever. 'I think I'm going to be sick.'

She was, violently, and afterwards she lay back

utterly spent and trembling while the Sister smoothed back the silky damp curls. 'Poor little girl!'

Sholto McNaughton turned back to her with a prepared injection in his hand. He held the needle up to the light, looked at it, then plunged it into the muscle of her arm.

'Oh, *don't*!' she cried out pitifully.

'I'm not going to let you suffer.'

'I'm going to die, aren't I?' Her pale, slender fingers suddenly clenched themselves around his wrist.

'No,' he answered emphatically, though he didn't raise the quiet tone one decibel. 'You've injured your head and you've broken your left leg. You know now I'm a doctor and I'm going to look after you.'

'I don't want anyone else.'

The other doctor moved nearer the table, observing her closely. 'Easy, lassie,' he said. 'Easy now. Hasn't he promised you he won't be going away?'

'I don't want anyone else,' she repeated, her voice becoming less and less audible.

'There's bleeding going on inside that delicate little skull,' Sholto McNaughton said bleakly when the girl was finally still.

'But the injury appears almost slight?' Tom Davenport looked across at his colleague, privately thinking the girl had been blessed by a small miracle. Sholto McNaughton was no ordinary doctor, nor did he usually frequent Casualty. He was a gifted neurosurgeon and honorary consultant to the hospital. He was, also, Tom Davenport's lifelong friend, which accounted for his presence in Casualty that morning.

Now Sholto's winged black brows were drawing together in a frown, a sure sign of impatience, perturbation. 'Call it intuition,' he said.

'Or your rare diagnostic talent. I wasn't questioning you, old chap.'

'God, so young!' Sholto was exclaiming. 'She scarcely looks more than a child.'

'Can't even remember her name.' Tom was taking a closer look at that small, matted wound. 'Brain scan?'

'Of course. Sister?' Sholto McNaughton turned away. 'Get a porter in here with a trolley.'

'Yes, Sir!' Sister answered promptly, and hurried away to take control.

'Poor little devil!' Tom was murmuring gently. 'The leg shouldn't be a problem—not a bad break at all. She must surely belong to someone, with a face like that. Nothing was on her to indicate a name or address, but the police are handling things.'

'She's English,' Sholto said, still frowning thoughtfully.

'Really? Such a shadow of a little voice I didn't notice.' Tom looked up startled, worried by the unusual tenseness of his friend's expression. 'What *is* it, Sholto?'

'She worries me,' Sholto returned tersely. 'Too bloody young to die.'

'She's got you,' Tom pointed out bracingly. 'Miracle worker.'

'Miracle worker nothing! All I can do is save a few.'

'Well, you would pick the most difficult and heartbreaking field of the lot.' Tom seized the other man's shoulder and shook it. 'I know you get violent when anyone calls you brilliant, but the fact is, you *are*. This little waif here is incredibly lucky. You're going to save her—and what's more, I'm sure you don't give a damn if you ever get paid.'

Sholto McNaughton paid no attention to him, concentrating on the small commotion outside the door. 'Here they come. Let's move her out of here, Tom.'

In the next instant, with a quick series of movements, Sister threw open the double doors and an orderly hurried through with a trolley.

CHAPTER TWO

A DOOR carefully opened and shut. The girl turned her head with an effort and saw a white figure move towards her.

'Ah, you're awake!'

Her vision became clear and she made an attempt to speak. Days in a hazy world had passed and her memory still eluded her. She searched the nurse's face. She was young and pretty with a quiet, gentle voice and gentle hands.

'I've been dreaming!' Marianne told her, and a glittering tear flowed down her face.

'Don't, dear.' The young nurse felt her own throat tighten and reached out a compassionate hand. 'You mustn't upset yourself. You've made a wonderful recovery and you've been so brave. Mr McNaughton will be in soon to see you. Try to be cheerful and just rest. You're over the worst of it and in no time you'll be your old self again. They say the operation was a miracle to watch. You were very, very lucky to have Mr McNaughton. He's a wonderful man and a brilliant surgeon.' The strong, gentle hands made Marianne comfortable and the nurse kept up a quiet, pleasant flow of words as she made her routine checks and wrote the results up on the chart that was secured to the end of Marianne's bed.

'Thank you. You're so kind to me. Everyone is.' Marianne lay back quietly, her small face haloed by bandages. 'I keep thinking every time I wake up, I'll remember who I am.'

'And you will, dear!' the nurse answered. 'You've been through a great deal and you must be patient. Mr McNaughton will explain to you that these things are gradual. Besides, we know who you are. You're Marianne Carroll. Such a pretty name, and it suits you! You're English and you've been in Australia for only a few months. These lovely flowers in the room have come from the people who work in your office, and everyone wants you to get well very soon. Mr McNaughton will say when you're to be allowed visitors.'

'And my family?' All this time Marianne's great smoky eyes had been fixed on the nurse's face.

'That's all I know, dear.' Nurse Mellors tried to smile. All of them felt immensely sympathetic and protective towards this pale little English girl who could remember nothing of her past life. 'I'm sure Mr McNaughton will have more news for you. He's taken a great interest in your case. Now, you must rest. You want him to be pleased with you, don't you?'

'Oh, *yes!*' A faint glow of colour lit the white and flawless skin. Of course she wanted him to be pleased with her. His was the only familiar face in the whole world, the only power. She turned her bandaged head along the pillow and willed herself back to sleep. Tomorrow, she told herself sadly, she would remember who she was and her foggy mind would become sharp and clear. Or did she want it to become clear? There was fear in her, a fantastic fear that sustained itself even when her memory was gone.

When Sholto McNaughton called that afternoon to see his patient, he found her out on the veranda, cushioned deeply in a wheelchair, the golden haze of sunlight playing over her small, triangular face and frail girl's body.

'Hello, Marianne, how are you?'

Sister Rogers, a cool, reserved woman, went to follow him out, but he waved her away. 'Thank you, Sister. I'll call, should I need you.'

'Yes, sir.' Sister withdrew respectfully, though she would have liked to stay. The girl was becoming too dependent on Mr McNaughton's visits. She had remarked it before—a tragic case that could lead to trouble. Sholto McNaughton was a strikingly handsome man and she knew the girl wasn't blind to it. The grey eyes were looking up at him with too obvious adoration.

'I was wondering if I'd see you today.' Marianne tried to sit up a little straighter, the fine bones of her face showing too sharply. Always feather-light, she looked positively breakable.

'Any more nightmares?' Sholto McNaughton sat opposite her, regarding her for a little time in silence.

'You've heard?' Marianne's delicate nostrils flared.

'Everything, Marianne. You know that. I'm your doctor.'

'You saved my life.'

'The good God spared your life. He just guided my hands.'

'The right hands,' she said emotionally. 'He gave the gift to the right man.' She glanced down at her own long slender fingers. 'Will I ever regain my memory?'

'Do you want to?' he asked oddly.

'But it matters terribly,' she said with a kind of blaze in her crystal eyes. '*Terribly*,' she repeated. 'I crave to know about my family. Surely I must have one. What am I doing in this country alone? How *old* am I?'

'Steady, Marianne,' he said quellingly when she looked as if she might burst into tears. 'I'm just wondering how much to tell you.'

'Then you know something?' She put out a hand to him convulsively.

'Yes,' he answered carefully. 'To begin, you're not Marianne Carroll, but her sister, Roslynn. You're nineteen years of age and you *do* have a family. Not an immediate family, but relatives.'

'And Marianne?' she asked eagerly.

'I'm very sorry, my dear.' He reached forward and took her two trembling hands in his own. 'Your sister died more than a year ago. You two girls were reared by your mother's cousin, a Mrs Vanessa Remington, and her husband Jeremy. They in turn have a son, to whom you were engaged.'

'*No!*'

'The facts are conclusive,' he said gently, pity in his sombre gaze. 'You must have been unhappy, Roslynn—disturbed over the death of your beloved sister. You ran away, took your sister's name and your mother's maiden name. Your real name is Ferrier, Roslynn Ferrier. Your father was the novelist Charles Ferrier and your parents were killed in a plane crash in South America when you were ten and your sister fourteen. Both of you were at boarding school in England and Mrs Remington came forward to care for you. After all, she'd been very close to your parents. She is, I believe, deeply distressed . . .'

'By my defection?' the young girl said bitterly.

'A strange word, Roslynn.' The far-seeing aquamarine eyes quizzed her. 'Have you remembered something?'

'No.' She shook her head. 'The words just surfaced from somewhere. I ran away—you told me.'

'People often do seemingly inexplicable things. I've been told you were suffering from a severe depression.'

'Yet I took the time off to become engaged?'

'It does sound a little remarkable,' he agreed. 'Then again, you're so young, so enormously young.

I expect you don't know what I mean. I can only tell you, Roslynn, what I've discovered about you so far. You have a family who are deeply concerned about you, your accident and your disappearance. They've conducted a search for you in the places you all knew in Europe. Your fiancé, so I've been told, is flying here to see you. It appears he was bereft when you disappeared.'

'Of course he loves me.' Again, the clear young voice was almost bitter.

'I imagine he does,' Sholto McNaughton said dryly. 'Well, Roslynn, you'll be a very beautiful girl.'

'You mean when my hair grows back.'

'It will very quickly,' he assured her. 'Don't worry about the little things, Roslynn.'

'I'm not,' she said apologetically. 'What you tell me simply takes my breath away.'

'I think you're strong enough to hear. In any case, your fiancé will be arriving in the next twenty-four hours.'

'I'm sure I've never been engaged in my life.'

'Why are you so sure?' He tilted her face back so she had to look at him.

'I *feel* sure,' she said doggedly, and tears sprang into her eyes. 'Call me mad if you want, but I don't want to see him.'

'How could it be otherwise?' he offered gravely. 'You're obviously afraid of something.' Brainwashed by fear, he thought, but didn't say. She *had* run away, and she didn't want to be reminded why. He had once had a patient—a young boy, who had confined himself to a wheelchair through sheer hysteria. He saw such strange things in his life's work: great bravery and phantom tumours that maimed. This child was so beautiful, so innocent, and she gave him the terrible feeling that what she might come out of was a nightmare. Whatever was causing this memory block it was unlikely it would remain for ever. Her memory *would* return, however slowly, or all at once.

She was sitting there quietly, letting his words sink in, grey eyes enormous, lips parted.

'What are you thinking?' he smiled at her rather tautly.

She released a little jagged breath. 'It's my own panic; I'm afraid of something ... someone. You sense it too.'

'We'll look after you, Roslynn,' he found himself saying. He had never seen eyes, a face, full of such intensity.

'Will you?' She was like a child, pleading. He almost had to turn away from those great, beseeching eyes. 'I'm so frightened!'

'I think you're very brave. It's an intolerable situation you're in, but you're escaping self-pity and hysteria. Every single day you're getting stronger. I'm really very pleased with you.'

'I owe you my life.' She looked down as she always did when she said it, twisting her small, pretty hands. 'Could I ask something more of you?'

'To be here when your fiancé comes?'

The flawless skin flushed. 'How do you always know what I'm going to say?'

'They tell me I'm intuitive.' He smiled at her and

she felt her heart give a violent lurch. How was it possible she was engaged, loved some man? All she knew was that she couldn't control what she felt for the man sitting so attentively opposite her. First his eyes, then his voice, then his hands. She knew from somewhere that women could be that way about their doctors. Not surprisingly, she supposed she was hopelessly in love with him—an emotional, manufactured kind of love, yet love all the same. Multiple feelings compounded of gratitude, endless gratitude, admiration for his skill and intelligence, the seduction of a wonderful face and body. For he *was* wonderful to look at. A Renaissance head, she thought, wondering why she retained such knowledge when the recollection of her family, her past life had fled.

She continued to stare at him and he seemed quite unaware of it. His eyes were startling with the black hair, slanted brows and thick, emphatic lashes. Then too, his skin was bronze. What time he had to himself, he obviously spent in the sun. But it was the bone structure she found so arresting, the hard, faintly hollow planes, the cleanness of line. His expression was rare, a mingling of compassion and a natural arrogance. He looked what he was, a very clever, highly professional man, a man who didn't suffer fools gladly but expected he would have to.

'Roslynn?' he queried with amused impatience.

'I'm sorry. Was I staring?'

'You were.' He narrowed his eyes at her.

'I'm so sorry,' she said again. 'You seem to be the only other human being I know.'

'It will all come back, Roslynn. You simply need time.'

'There are so many levels of the mind,' she mused.

'Yes,' he agreed quietly. So many manifestations of fear and inadequacies.

All of a sudden she looked very tired. 'I realise I'm acting as though I'm very dependent on you, I know.'

'I'm certainly not worried, Roslynn.'

'Sister Rogers is,' she said dryly.

He stood up, obviously amused by her observation. 'Just rest and be thankful you've come through everything so well. I have to hurry now. I have a consultation in the next half-hour.'

'Thank you for coming.' She lifted her grey eyes.

'If you think it will help, I'll endeavour to be here when Remington arrives,' he told her.

'I wish I could remember him.' She said it not wistfully, not violently.

'Perhaps you will all at once.'

'Then we'll know by tomorrow.' It was an effort to keep emotion out of her voice.

'Goodbye, Roslynn,' he said, taking her hand with a warm, comforting touch.

'Goodbye, Mr McNaughton.'

'So serious?'

'Please *be* here,' she said.

She was lying very sick and quietly when Sister O'Hare showed a slender, studiedly elegant young man into her room. His hair was golden and immaculately groomed and Roslynn had never seen him before in her life.

'Rosa!' he said brokenly, and came to the side of the bed.

She was aware that she had recoiled sharply, yet how could anyone recoil from such a golden young man? 'I'm sorry.' She was trying hard, too hard, to remember.

'Darling!' He bent his head and kissed her cheek tenderly, winning all Sister O'Hare's sympathy in an instant. 'You must tell me everything that's happened.'

Where's Mr McNaughton? she thought wildly. Without him I can't manage. I shall go mad. Above her head Sister O'Hare was cooing, offering a chair, and the golden haired young man had turned to her, a smile lighting his smooth face.

'Thank you so much.'

'I'll leave you alone for the moment,' Sister said. 'I believe Mr McNaughton will be along to have a word with you, Mr Remington.'

'Ah, yes, the surgeon!'

'Our best,' Sister O'Hare nodded amiably, delighted the little English girl's fiancé had turned out to be so nice.

'I'd like to see him,' the young man said confidently. 'Thank him for all he's done for Roslynn.'

'Oh, quite.' Sister's tone implied that Mr McNaughton had saved Roslynn's life.

After she had gone, Roslynn stared blankly into the watchful hazel eyes. 'You've been told, I know, that I've lost my memory.'

'Darling, it will come back,' he comforted her with acute concern.

'I hope so.' She glanced away from him, quite unmoved by a young man she was supposed to have loved.

'Mother and Father send their love.' He sounded considerably shaken. 'Can you imagine how we all felt when you ran off?'

'That's the trouble,' she said, 'I can't.'

He gave her a brooding look. 'Then it really is true, this line about amnesia?'

'Ask Mr McNaughton,' she said, going white.

'What's he like?' He was staring down into her face alertly and she heard herself giving a great sigh.

'He saved my life.'

'I expect that's his job. What else?' The good-looking, boyish face flushed slightly.

'See him for yourself.'

'That sounds like you, Roslynn,' he said, narrowing his eyes. 'What makes this all so tricky is that you're a very good actress.'

'You mean you don't believe me?' she demanded.

'Suppose I say I don't. Darling, don't forget I've known you all your life. Why, you're the most fascinating little creature alive—the things you say and the things you do. The way you *pretend*.'

'I'm not pretending now,' she said quietly.

'I wonder.' He picked up one of her hands and touched it to his cheek. 'You won't get away from me you know, Ros. There's nobody for me but you, and I will make you happy.'

'But I don't know you,' she uttered a funny little cry. 'I mean, I've forgotten.'

'Sweetheart, the whole thing is one of your little jokes.'

'No.' She felt she must be crying.

'I'm not suggesting I'm angry with you. Not any more. I've come to take you back home. Together we'll fill in all the little pieces. You've always been impulsive, unpredictable. I mean, this whole thing is unmistakably *you*.'

'To bring such misery on myself!' she sighed.

'Oh—not that,' he glanced at her bandaged head. 'But this mysterious amnesia is just the sort of thing you would do. You always were a dramatic little thing. Fighting and accusing and making difficulties, but so lovely I can't look at another girl.'

'Please don't touch me.' Her skin seemed to be crawling.

'There's no need to be afraid of me.' He stared at her with darkened hazel eyes, lifting her hand and clasping it tenderly. 'Oh, Rosa, you *do* love me. Just because Marianne came between us. . . .'

The sound of the name upset her so dreadfully she pulled away urgently. 'Marianne, my sister?'

'Listen, Rosa, cut it out,' he spoke sharply. 'I realise what you're up to. You've been playing games since you were a child. Probably you got all that drama from your father.'

'I can't remember him either.' She laughed wildly.

He looked alarmed and put one hand on her fragile shoulder. 'For God's sake. . . . There's nothing to be gained by all this. When you're well enough to travel, I just want to take you home.'

'I won't go.'

'You will, sweetheart, don't delude yourself. Now let's forget the antics and talk.' The boyish face looked wary and watchful and cynical. 'I never was to blame for what happened to Marianne. You know that, and you've punished me enough.'

'What happened to her, exactly?' The tears stood in her beautiful eyes.

'Remember, Rosa, all your games were dangerous.'

'Then I thank God I can't remember them.' The pounding in her head was terrible, and as his fingers bit into her shoulder a man's figure loomed up in the doorway and he spoke, his voice cutting across the silence with severe authority.

'*Mr Remington!*'

The young man looked more than startled. He dropped his hand and stood up. 'I beg your pardon.'

'You must be aware,' McNaughton said curtly, 'your fiancée must be treated gently.'

'Of course.' The young man looked sullen and intimidated at once. 'It's just that I reject this theory of amnesia.'

'You surprise me,' the surgeon said coolly, crossing to Roslynn's bed, picking up her hand and checking her pulse. 'My name's McNaughton, by the way.'

'I reckoned you must be,' the young man waited for Sholto McNaughton to accept his outstretched hand. 'Kenneth Remington.'

'How do you do.' Instead of smiling, the surgeon frowned. 'I'm afraid I'll have to cut your visit short.'

'I'd greatly appreciate it if you wouldn't,' Kenneth

Remington protested. 'I've flown fourteen thousand miles to be with Rosa.'

'Then you must be completely exhausted.'

'I really am damned sorry if I've upset her.'

'I expect you don't fully appreciate what she's been through.' Sholto McNaughton's voice resembled his appearance, formidable in the extreme. 'For the moment I think I had better answer all your questions.'

'You really believe this amnesia is real?' Quite shockingly Kenneth Remington laughed.

'Not only real but hellish, I should think.'

'You don't know Rosa.' Kenneth Remington's voice implied that he knew everything about the girl there was to know.

'I certainly know her physical condition,' Sholto McNaughton said coldly.

'I don't know you,' Roslynn whispered behind them, her small face strained almost beyond endurance. 'Please believe me—I don't know you.'

'To be honest, Doctor,' Kenneth Remington said pleasantly, 'Roslynn always was an impressive little actress. Her father wasn't merely an accomplished writer, he was brilliant. Roslynn takes after him, with all her fantasies.'

'At the moment that isn't the problem,' Sholto McNaughton's dark voice dripped ice. He pressed the call button to summon a nurse, then placed a compelling hand on the young man's shoulder. 'I suggest we discuss this outside. I can use any one of several offices.'

'I'd like it even better to stay with Rosa,'

Remington tried to extricate his shoulder, but couldn't.

'Please, Mr Remington, another time.' The surgeon impelled the younger man into the corridor, stopping to give a few instructions to Sister O'Hare who was hurrying to obey the summons of the call-button.

'He doesn't believe me!' Roslynn was so disturbed she blurted the words out to Sister at once.

'Hush, dear,' Sister muttered, seeing all trace of colour had drained from the girl's face. 'Mr McNaughton thinks you need a sedative.'

'No, I want to talk to him.'

'Your fiancé?' Sister looked perplexed.

'I don't *know* my fiancé!' The huge grey eyes were full of tears. 'I want to speak to Mr McNaughton. He's the only one who can tell me what to do.' Roslynn caught Sister's arm, clasping it at the wrist.

'Please, dear,' Sister implored, then relented. 'Mr McNaughton will come back to check on you. At the moment he's speaking to your visitor.'

'I don't mean to be a bother.' After the needle Roslynn's voice sounded vague.

'You're no bother at all. You're a good patient,' Sister said softly.

'Will this put me out?'

'No, just make you feel calmer.' How atrocious that that nice boy could have so upset her. Sometimes it happened that way no matter how well intentioned the visitor.

Roslynn kept her eyes open until Sholto McNaughton returned.

'Just as I thought,' he said mildly. 'Still awake?'

'I want to hear what you told him.'

'I told him it was too bad he upset you.' He approached the bed and stood there looking down at her.

'I obviously upset him as well?'

'Yes,' he admitted after a moment. 'There's no possibility you'll be fit to travel for a month or so.'

'God forbid!' She actually shuddered with fervour.

'You don't want to go back to England?'

Out of nowhere she had a vision of an enormous Venetian chandelier. 'Oh!' she said, like a little stab of pain.

'What is it?' His eyes were alert, though his face remained impassive.

'I just had a flash of memory.' She shivered visibly. 'A huge, sparkling chandelier—Venetian. I used to see it every day.'

'But you don't remember where?'

'No. It just slipped in and out of my mind like that.' She made a little clicking motion of her fingers.

'You don't remember your fiancé at all?'

Was there a trace of scepticism in his face? 'No,' she said quietly. 'Not one single feature. Not his eyes or his mouth or the colour of his hair.'

'Then we have no means of telling whether he really is your fiancé beyond what he says?'

'I suppose not.' She turned her head drowsily. 'I couldn't forget *your* eyes, I'm sure.'

He looked completely unruffled by such a personal observation. 'It's not the proper time to discuss it all now. For the moment, your physical wellbeing is my sole concern. When you're stronger and if your

memory doesn't return spontaneously I'll arrange for
you to see a good friend of mine. He may be able to
help you unlock the past.'

'What if it's unwelcome?' she asked, and suddenly
opened her shadowy eyes.

'You forget I've had a talk with . . . Remington.
There's no cause for fear.'

'Yet I'm deadly frightened.' She was muttering,
almost to herself.

'Now close your eyes, Roslynn,' he said. 'Your
eyelids are growing heavier and heavier.'

Because they were so very long, her lashes lay like
dark silken fans on her pale cheeks. She looked so
excessively fragile he still had difficulty concealing
his anger. Stephen Remington's approach had been
totally self-centred, insensitive, yet he had protested
for the most part how deeply he loved the girl. He
had maintained as well this theory of amnesia was a
fiction. He had known this sleeping girl all his life.
She had always been prone to play-acting, highly
strung. She had certainly run away from her family
and made their life barren.

Sholto McNaughton looked down at the exquisite
little face, trying to see past its beauty to the brain
beneath. Was it possible she was lying, or had her
mind really cringed away from her past? Either way,
he intended to find out.

CHAPTER THREE

ROSLYNN saw Kenneth Remington many more times before she left hospital, but each time he was careful not to upset her. It wasn't his own idea not to probe her curiously remote state, but Sholto McNaughton's. Sholto McNaughton, the great man. Kenneth had met very few men like McNaughton and for that he was considerably relieved. He disliked the man intensely, but for all that he was profoundly wary of crossing him. Mother would have to do that.

It seemed, at least, he was able to tell Roslynn that. She was looking much better, he observed, with a tinge of pretty colour in her cheeks but no glorious rose-leaf bronzed hair to frame her triangular face. In spite of everything, her operation and Sholto McNaughton's assurances, he was convinced this senseless loss of memory story was just something she had concocted to hurt him and make him angry. At times he even thought she really hated him.

He began by taking her hand gently. 'McNaughton told me I might tell you Mother is flying here so we can all be together until you're well enough to come home.'

'I don't know what your mother looks like. Tell me.'

'That's not easy to believe, Rosa,' he said, shocked.

'But in my case, the truth.' The tender mouth twisted in an ironic smile. 'Believe me, I'm finding it as amazing as you are. I can't conjure up anything of places and personalities. I've turned into an oddity.'

She did look very intense, her shimmery grey eyes swallowing up her face. 'You know what *I* look like,' he said. 'I resemble Mother a good deal. We both have fair hair and hazel eyes. I can show you a picture of Mother if you like.'

'Thank you,' Roslynn said tonelessly.

From his wallet he took out a shiny colour photograph and she took it, staring at it with an absorption she had not shown in Kenneth's presence.

The woman in the photograph was standing posed beside a motor car. She was very slim, fashionably dressed, but Roslynn didn't recognise her. She recognised the car; it was a Rolls-Royce.

'What a nice car!' she said brightly so that she wouldn't cry.

'Of course you remember when we bought it. What a celebration *that* was! Almost two years to the day.'

'Two years,' said Roslynn, sick with all the emptiness inside her.

'They aren't all that cheap,' Kenneth smiled. 'But Mother thought it was time to match the house.'

'Has it got a chandelier?'

'Hell, dozens,' Kenneth exclaimed. He swung his golden-blond head upright and stared at her. 'Don't tell me you've forgotten your own home?'

'One wouldn't think so,' she said unsteadily.

He shook her head. 'No. It's scarcely the sort of place one forgets. Your father paid a fortune for it.

Of course he made plenty in those early days. The books are still paying off.'

'You mean it's *my* house?' she asked, bemused.

'Of course it's your house,' he said, thoroughly irritated. 'That's why we all considered it so strange your running off. Mother had people searching everywhere, but strange to say she never thought of Australia. I mean, it's so damned far away, and so *hot*. I dislike heat and brilliant sunlight.'

'What do you think of amnesia?'

'Too much to swallow,' Kenneth chuckled quietly. 'All right, so you've put up a brave fight against the nasty relatives. You know now we really love you and we've always had your best interests at heart. I suppose Mother is, in a sense, domineering, but she's never been one to sit back and let people make mistakes. As for Marianne, frail as she was, she always was a bad influence over you. Well, neither of you had it easy, orphaned like that, but you certainly weren't left paupers. . . .'

'Are you trying to tell me I'm rich?'

'Born rich, inherited rich,' he said almost bitterly. 'Marianne was always sounding off about how it was *your* money, instead of thanking Mother for all she'd done. Who else came forward to look after you?'

'I don't know,' said Roslynn.

'God, Rosa,' Kenneth shook his head irritably, 'are you going to write a book about it or something?'

'To be honest, I'm going under hypnosis.'

'I bet you've got a lot to say for yourself, then. It's terrible, your imagination.'

'Too much?'

'You said yourself that when you had enough experience of life you were going to write a novel. I guess it's in your blood.' He reached forward and picked up her hand, carrying it to his mouth. 'Let's forget everything that's happened and just be happy. We used to be in the old days. What you have never understood about Marianne is that she was jealous—jealous of your looks and health and your love of life. She was even jealous about me, though I don't want to talk about it, it was so horrible.'

'How did Marianne die?' She spoke in a remote way, her grey eyes raying right through him.

'Oh, stop it, Ros!'

'I want to know.'

'Does it give you some kind of weird pleasure doing this?' he demanded.

'I doubt if losing one's memory is a pleasure. You must accept that I really don't know.'

Kenneth shook his head and his voice sank to a near whisper. 'Marianne died in a tragic accident. A group of us went swimming in the lake, the water was cold, but it didn't bother any of us except Marianne. By the time we found her it was too late.'

'How dreadful!' Something glimmered at the edges of her mind but refused to pervade her brain.

'Dreadful, yes.' He put his head in his hands. 'You were so frantic, so grief-stricken, you had to be put out. I still have the scar where you clawed me. It was never my fault, Rosa, I did everything I could. Marianne was always trying to squeeze things out of life. Things she couldn't do.'

There was a terrible tenseness inside her. 'And afterwards, I ran away?'

'No, not immediately. Gradually you seemed to settle down, but I suppose all kinds of resentments became wedged in your mind. You turned on us all—accused us as Marianne did of being parasites. God, to say *that* to Mother! Small wonder she retaliated, and Mother has never struck anyone in her life.'

'I take it she's forgiven me?' Roslynn gave a strange little smile.

'She loves you dearly,' Kenneth said in his soft voice. 'You were always the sweet one, the one with the affection and the gaiety. Marianne resented us from the beginning. She never did fit in.'

'It seems to me she didn't have to, in her own home.'

He raised his head abruptly, brushing his hand across his eyes. 'There you go again!' he accused her. 'How can I believe you've lost your memory when you sound exactly the same?'

When he had gone, Roslynn lay there quietly trying to pierce the darkness of her mind. She even clutched her fragile body, holding herself in, desperately willing herself to remember. It was like being blind, quite alone in the dark. Surely a single blow, no matter how serious the complications had been, couldn't cause this total loss of the past? A sister's death one could accept as a tremendous emotional shock, and much more terrible a blow if an element of guilt had been involved. Sholto (she was already calling him Sholto in her mind) had told her em-

phatically that there had been no actual changes in
her brain, so the moment of truth, the day of recall,
would happen, or could be *made* to happen. She could
be treated by hypnosis or by drugs. Either way she
instinctively rejected. It was her mind and she didn't
want it invaded. She was even frightened by what
they might learn. Kenneth had pointed out many
times how 'imaginative' she was. Not in any good
sense, but more a person who invented things and
situations. She didn't think she was like that, but
how would she really know? Besides, there was an
enormous difference between high melodrama and
the death of a beloved sister. Her head was beginning
to ache slightly. For the time being she would have
to relax.

'I'm sorry, I woke you,' a voice said.

'Oh, hello!' She was unable to keep the vibrancy
out of her face or her tone.

He picked up her chart and stared down at it for a
few moments. 'Keep improving as you do and we
won't be able to keep you.'

'But where can I go?' Her heart twisted over. This
stranger, her doctor, she would miss all her life.

'That's what I want to talk to you about, Roslynn.'
He turned a chair around and sat down. 'I would
recommend a period of some six to eight weeks before
you take up normal life again.'

'That's not easy when I've no place to go.'

'You haven't considered going home?'

Roslynn shut her eyes hard trying to capture that
sparkling chandelier again, but it wouldn't come.

'Please tell me what you're thinking,' asked Sholto.

'I'm trying to see that chandelier again,' she said simply, 'but I can't will anything to come.'

'If you really want to unlock doors, Roslynn, you'll have to consider hypnosis,' he told her.

'I'd be too scared,' she said in a hushed, lost tone. 'I suppose Kenneth has told you everything?'

'As much as it's necessary for me to know. He told me all about the tragic death of your sister.'

Marianne. The name screamed inside her.

'What *is* it?' He sensed her torture before he actually saw it.

'Oh.' She lay back with the cold sweat breaking out on her temples.

'Some memory?' He had her hand.

'More a finger of pain.' Her young face had a heartbreaking, abandoned air, and she shut her eyes as his fingers touched her forehead. And there was the power again, overcoming the pain and the darkness. 'How wonderful,' she sighed quietly, 'you can drive away pain at a touch.'

'I'm beginning to believe it,' his voice had an attractive break in it. 'I would recommend hypnosis for you, Roslynn. We won't let it become too unbearable.'

'Does it always work?' She opened her eyes again, staring up at him.

'If you genuinely want to know. My friend Doctor Pirelli has a high rate of success.'

'You wouldn't let me go on my own?'

'Roslynn,' he looked down into her grey eyes, 'I don't know if it's good, all this faith you have in me.'

'You mean I'm becoming too dependent on you? I

know.' She could almost see Sister Rogers' disapproval.

'And I, too, am duly aware of it.'

'I'm sorry.' She turned her head away, the delicate skull covered with a fine dark red down like a baby's.

'However,' he continued, 'I'm more than usually involved in your case.'

'Of course, the circumstances. . . .'

'Don't flirt with me, Roslynn,' he said unexpectedly.

'But I'm not . . . I'd *never!*'

'Are you asking me to ignore how you're using your eyes?' Laconically he raised one black, winged eyebrow. 'Never mind. That's nothing unusual in a female.'

'I'll be frightened now to look at you at all,' she sighed.

'That's all right, little one, I won't let you get away with it.' He was amused and smiling, an indulgent adult to a child. 'How is the rapport between you and your fiancé?'

'Don't call him that,' she said, quite definitely.

'Well, he calls himself that,' he replied.

'Where's my ring?' She held up a small, beautifully shaped hand.

'Haven't you asked him?' He was serious behind the sardonic look.

'I ask him very little, which is very curious. I can't even think I like him.'

'Well, he most assuredly loves you.'

'Is that your honest opinion?' She tried to hold those aquamarine eyes.

Wants you, he thought, but didn't say, unimpressed with Kenneth Remington himself. 'Surely that's the reason people become engaged?'

'Have you ever been engaged?' she asked.

'Please don't hesitate to ask more.'

'I'm sorry,' she apologised again. 'You don't have to answer any of my ridiculous questions.'

'I was engaged once, Roslynn. It didn't work out. I've always been far too interested in my career.'

'And it's a good one, a great one,' she said almost fiercely. 'Do you think you could find out something about my background in England? Not through Kenneth or his mother but through some agency. I know I ask a lot of you, but I have no one else to ask. They tell me I'm rich, or rich enough. I can pay for it all later.'

'I've already found out quite a bit, Roslynn,' he told her.

'But you never *told* me!'

'I invariably watch your condition.' He settled into his highly professional look, a mask to cloak a disturbingly attractive man. 'Everything is very much as Remington told me. You are the sole owner of a very beautiful country house in Sussex left to you and your sister by your late father. After your parents were killed your guardian, Mrs Remington, sold up her own property and moved into the house with you girls. You did become engaged to Kenneth Remington on your eighteenth birthday. I've learned that your sister Marianne was very much against it.'

'Why?'

'I would say she thought you too young.'

'*And?*' She searched his eyes as though she was looking for some fathomless secret.

'And we'll leave it at there for the time being.' He jerked his dark head up to look at the clock. 'I should have been away from here ten minutes ago.'

'You lead a very frantic life,' she commented. 'It's not good for you.'

'I know that.' His beautiful mouth twisted in a smile. 'Doctors usually finish up feeling exhausted. What I want to tell you, Roslynn, is, you have a friend. If you decide not to go back to England immediately, I can arrange for you to stay with my grandmother. She lives all alone in our old family house and I know she would be very glad of your company. Better yet, she too was a doctor. She'll be able to keep an eye on you.'

'But how *kind*!' The tears sprang into her eyes.

'It will leave me feeling a whole lot better. When you've recovered your memory completely you'll be able to face up better to life, to your own situation.'

'Yes.' Her face expressed her inevitable sadness. 'No one can *make* me go home, can they?'

'Of course not. As it happens, they seem determined on helping you, but until we've got you out of your trauma I think it better for you to stay put.'

'Then I'm going to yield to your great kindness and go home to your grandmother.'

'I'll tell her,' Sholto smiled slightly into her shadowed eyes, watching that fragile body subside in solace.

When Kenneth heard about the plan, he was furious. 'What right has McNaughton got to interfere?' his mouth thinned. '*I'm* here, and Mother will be here the day after tomorrow. We're your family.'

'I just don't have a family at the moment,' Roslynn said. 'Please try to understand.'

'No never! I'm going to have a word with this McNaughton fellow. He might be the great man around this hospital, but that doesn't cut any ice with me.'

'I thought you found him quite daunting,' Roslynn responded.

'He strikes me as a very arrogant devil indeed. Who is he to make plans for you?'

'I'm by no means cured, Kip,' she said gently.

They were sitting out in the cool of the wide corridor and he jumped up in agitation, his demeanour almost violent. 'You called me Kip!' he said vehemently. 'That was a slip, wasn't it, darling?'

Roslynn felt as though she couldn't breathe. 'It just surfaced from nowhere.'

'This is agony, Ros,' he said, returning to his seat close beside her. 'How long can you keep blaming me? I swear I never heard Marianne call. How *could* you believe it?' His strong young hands swept up and clutched her shoulders. 'Why don't you tell him the truth? You haven't lost your memory at all. You just want to shut your mind on what happened. I understand, darling, but we can't wreck what we had. You were meant for me from the beginning. The parents were overjoyed at our engagement. Surely you can't play that down. We were happy, Ros, and we will be again.'

'You're hurting me,' she protested.

'Sorry.' He looked grim. 'Please don't go with McNaughton. He seems to possess some power over you.'

'I trust him.'

'Meaning you don't trust me?'

The realisation made her stand up albeit a little waveringly. 'I must have *time*, Kenneth.'

'Kip,' he corrected her bitterly. 'You can't pretend to forget everything so easily.'

Roslynn felt pity rise in her, but there was no way she was going with him on her present instincts. 'Mr McNaughton wants me to have further treatment,' she said.

'What fun you'll have with a psychiatrist.'

She sank back into the armchair because she had to. 'Perhaps by some miracle I'll regain my memory without one, but I don't think so.'

'I want you with me,' he said passionately. 'You've brought me all this way, and Mother will be arriving. It can't be all for nothing. So you need time to recuperate, convalesce. We'll rent a place. The thing is, you can't be left to yourself to sit in a room and mope. That's what you did before.'

'Didn't I work?' she asked sharply.

'*Work?*' he all but snorted. 'Why would *you* have to work? You wanted to, of course, and Marianne kept droning on about your independence, but once we got engaged the matter sort of dropped.'

'And what do *you* do?' she asked.

'You know damned well what I do,' he said wearily. 'I put in my day with Dad.'

'And that is? Tell me, I'm curious.'

'I always knew you were high-spirited, but I never knew you were cruel,' he snapped.

'It makes me just as sad to know you don't believe me.'

'It's hard when you look so incongruously innocent.' Kenneth moved his head and the light caught the gold of his hair.

'I have to go back to my room,' she said, wondering if she would ever come out of this nightmare. She felt tired and drained, unable to cope with the wealth of information pressing down on her. Visions, like a mirage, kept shimmering on the far horizons of her brain, but they never advanced, just remained there to never quite infiltrate the territory of her mind. She would have to come out of this or go mad.

She was discharged from hospital the following day and in the cool of the afternoon Sholto drove her to the old McNaughton summer residence on Montclair, a spur of the dividing range, and about an hour's drive from the city. It was strange to be driving in a car, no longer in a hospital gown. Roslynn glanced down at the lovely, cool dress she was wearing wondering which particular friend of his had supplied her with a suitcase full of clothes. A woman, of course, and a woman who recognised quality as she realised she must do herself. She would have to fully face up to the fact that a man like Sholto McNaughton would have many friends, male and female. She had seen the way the nurses looked at him. Even Sister Rogers wrecked her own inviolate image by blushing whenever she gained his attention.

'You look very delicate,' he said lightly, 'like a princess.'

'I still haven't thanked you properly for my clothes. How did you know all the sizes?'

'Oh, Roslynn,' he said dryly.

'Well, you surely didn't pick them?'

'No, Laura did that.'

'Do you want to tell me who Laura is?' she asked.

'A good friend of mine.'

'Do you love her?'

He turned his dark head briefly to glance at her. 'Don't sound so heartbroken!'

'Do I?' She wished she didn't depend on him as the only other person in the world.

'Roslynn,' he said, and his voice was unbearably gentle, 'don't fall in love with me. I can't help you if you fall in love with me.'

'Oh, please,' she tilted her head back and tears crept into her huge, luminous eyes.

'Promise.' His hand moved to hers in her lap, clenched briefly.

'Would it be so terribly bad?'

'Yes, little one, it would.'

'Because you love Laura and it would be an embarrassment?'

'Because it would be wrong for you.'

'Well, I'll do my best,' she said, and a faint smile came into his eyes, softening the austerity of his handsome face.

'Until your memory comes back it might be as well to allow your emotions a rest.

'Don't worry,' she bent her delicate head. 'A lot of

women lose their hearts to their doctors, but it doesn't mean anything.'

For answer he laughed, a deep amused murmur in his throat. 'I should feel a crisis has been averted, instead I feel almost let down.'

'Is Laura a doctor too?' she asked, turning her rose-petalled head towards him.

'Laura, my inquisitive child, is the widow of a former colleague of mine.'

'But she was always in love with you and it was useless at the time.'

'Words fail me,' he sighed.

'So I'm right?' She looked out the window at the great beauty of the scenery.

'Do you want me to turn you over my knee?'

Yes, she thought, and for a moment there was a curious stillness between them. 'I should mind my own business, I know,' she said shakily, 'but I can't think of anything of my own. I can't believe I even existed before now.'

'Okay,' Sholto said briskly, 'we won't dwell on it. I'm going to stop the car a little further on. There's a splendid vantage point to look down over the valley.'

'It's all very beautiful,' she said, dazzled by the green and blue and gold of this wondrous world. It was the hour before twilight and heat still shimmered across the bonnet of the car, but inside the Daimler it was pleasurably cool. Roslynn knew the car, the interior, the ride. She was quite sure, if she had to, she could drive it. She had felt a steering wheel like that before in her hands. She even had a fleeting sensation of the lightness of the steering, the purring power beneath her hands.

'I can drive this car,' she told him, her heart beating faster.

'We won't try it out on the mountain.' His eyes against the darkness of his skin were brilliantly alive.

'Some time?'

'Poor child, yes.' They swept around a curve, then he turned the long, elegant bonnet towards a small clearing which was obviously a lookout. 'I love this part of the country,' he said. 'It has that special magic that's part of great physical beauty and the scene of a wonderfully happy childhood. Every summer holiday we used to pack up and come up here to the mountain. The house has become much too big, but we're too fond of it to tear it down and build something more suitable for today. A lot of the rooms are closed up, but you can have a lot of fun exploring.'

'Your grandmother doesn't find it too lonely on her own?' They were out of the car and and he was guiding her, one hand beneath her elbow.

'She has a garden to fill her heart when I'm not here. A very beautiful garden, I might add. Then too, we have a caretaker and his wife. Bill helps my grandmother in the garden and Annie manages the house. It's an arrangement that's gone on remarkably well for the past ten years. I didn't care for my grandmother living alone.'

'You're a very caring person,' Roslynn observed.

'Don't dwell too much on my attributes. I have lots of faults.'

'Yes,' she said, and sounded a little bit reckless.

'You *could* be very impatient and on occasion rather deliciously arrogant.'

'It's a long drop down,' he warned.

'I'm not afraid of heights.' Indeed her cheeks were flushed and there was a brilliance in her crystal eyes.

The wind was streaming joyously around them and the air was so fresh and cool, laden with many fragrances.

'One should put a temple up on this spot,' said Roslynn.

'The valley is beautiful in this light. When I'm tired or depressed I try and conjure it up.'

'It can't be easy to be a doctor. You must see many things that fill you with sadness.'

'And revulsion,' he sighed faintly. 'In my profession it's always the season for dying.'

She heard the strong feeling in his voice, though his tone was very quiet. 'You saved *me*.'

He looked down at her. 'I really don't know what I would have done if I hadn't.'

It was a brief moment but very deep, but then, as though determined to reassert the proper relationship, he began to point out landmarks. The hills and the valley were clothed in trees, young grass and wildflowers, houses that were transmuted by the extraordinary light into sculptures. Roslynn leaned forward quickly and he held her. 'You can only look, Roslynn, not climb down.'

'It's a wonderful sight.'

'I agree.'

She turned her head expectantly in another direction, her pulses singing under the warm clasp of his hand. The magnificent stands of eucalypts fascinated her, reaching up to mighty heights. It was very much cooler here than down on the lowlands and the greenness of the vegetation was almost iridescent. It reminded her of other woodlands, other scenes to delight the heart. Far off there was a silver shimmer, a clear sheet of water, and staring at it she suddenly turned rigid with fear. Messages of alarm flashed to her brain and tremors brushed the entire length of her body.

'Roslynn, are you okay?' His voice sounded very far off.

She was poised precariously not on a mountainside but the brink of cognition, the valley beneath her wavering giddily, yet her staring eyes concentrated on that shining lake of water. There was a noise in her ears like the beating of a hundred wings rendering her deaf to the question Sholto was asking her so grimly. With his arms locked around her now she gave a broken little cry, then as the moment passed her, collapsed against him like a spent, exhausted child.

'Let me take you back to the car.'

She tried to nod her head, but the effort seemed too much. And then he lifted her right into his arms, cradling her insubstantial weight, on his own face an expression of strain.

'What happened?' he asked her when she was almost totally herself.

'I . . . I don't know.' Her voice sounded frightened.

'You all but passed out.' His fingers were cool now on her wrist.

'You don't think I'm going mad, do you?'

'I know you've been through a good deal. Don't talk for the moment, Roslynn. All this stress is no good.'

'I expect you're sorry you've brought me now.'

'I *said*, stay quiet.'

'Yes, Doctor, though it's *Mr* McNaughton, isn't it?'

'What am I to make of you, Roslynn,' he sighed. 'Is your head aching?'

'Slightly.'

'I'll get you home.'

Her eyes fastened rather desperately on his strong, chiselled profile. 'Thank God *you're* real!'

They continued the rest of the journey in complete silence, Sholto considering further treatment, or a form of treatment that would be best for her, she looking and feeling utterly exhausted.

The great house loomed up, three stories high in a very grand design, but for all its overall size it stirred up warm feelings of welcome. The trees she knew were all there, oaks, elms, beeches, they had come through an avenue of poplars and the extensive gardens were in glorious flower.

'I think I expected something as beautiful as this,' she told him.

'Don't talk, Roslynn,' he said quietly. 'Save your strength.'

'But what will your grandmother think?'

'My grandmother will *know*.' He stopped the car in front of the splendid white portico and she looked

out the window up the broad flight of steps to the
open front door. Inside the entrance hall a chandelier
was glowing, spilling its radiance into a lofty space.

'Duck your head.' Instead of helping her out, he
lifted her bodily, balancing her for a second as he
looked up at the windows of the second floor.

'Coming, darling!' a voice called.

Roslynn's grey eyes widened. 'Your grandmother?'

'There must be close on a dozen women who call
me darling, but yes, it's my grandmother. Try to
relax, Roslynn. You're a bundle of quivering nerves.'

Her first sight of Elizabeth McNaughton calmed
her immediately. Here was a woman from whom
strength, warmth and understanding flowed out in a
bright stream. She began immediately to show them
up the stairway to the beautiful big bedroom that
had been made ready for her young guest.

'It's an exhausting day, the first day out of hospital.' Swiftly and efficiently she turned back the silk
bedcover while her grandson lowered Roslynn on to
a beautiful old mahogany fourposter that dwarfed
her. 'Now, what happened?'

'A near-faint.'

'I can see that.' Elizabeth McNaughton nodded
and turned away from her grandson to place her
hand on Roslynn's forehead. 'You know that we're
going to get you well, don't you?'

'Yes, I know.' Roslynn smiled in recognition.
Elizabeth McNaughton, in her seventies, was still a
handsome woman, silver-haired, dark-eyed, standing
upright and tall, eyes and rather deep, resonant voice

saying *welcome.* 'Thank you very much for having me.'

'I'm delighted you're here,' Elizabeth told her without hesitation. 'I've always found the mountain air enormously beneficial.'

'It's my head,' Roslynn said wryly. 'I can't remember anything.'

'Poor child,' Elizabeth answered her cheerfully. 'But it will come back, my dear, bank on that. Maybe not tomorrow, but when you've put on some weight and you're feeling a whole lot better in yourself.'

'Better get her some tea, then,' Sholto laughed.

'Oh, it's lovely to have you!' Elizabeth grasped her tall, handsome grandson in a strong, lively clasp. 'I can't imagine what I'd do without your visits.'

'You wouldn't consider emigrating to the city?'

'Never—and leave my garden?' Her voice became suddenly serious. 'You're not going to rush back, are you?'

'Darling, I have to.'

'You work too hard, Sholto,' she told him.

'Yes, love.'

'You must always remember overwork killed your father.'

'Don't worry, I'll be around a long time.' Sholto moved to the bed and looked down at Roslynn alertly. 'Feeling better?'

'Fine.' In truth the weak sickness had disappeared. 'May I get up now?'

'No, you may not.'

'Do I need your permission?'

Elizabeth McNaughton looked startled, then burst out laughing. 'How about that, Sholto? I think this child might be good for you.'

'I'm pretty sure she'll be a handful after a few weeks of your care.'

'What did you expect when you brought me a redhead?' His grandmother smiled at him. 'When have redheads ever been nice and easy?'

Sholto gave his rare but beautiful smile. 'At least she's a country girl. Very much country. She shows her pleasure in her face.'

'So much the better!' Elizabeth looked pleased. 'Then I'm sure she'll have a wonderful time discovering the garden.'

CHAPTER FOUR

THERE were only two days of respite before Roslynn had to make herself ready to greet Kenneth and the woman she had once called Aunt Vanessa.

'I'm absolutely petrified,' she told Elizabeth as they sat out in the walled rose-garden.

'Do you know *why* exactly, dear?' Elizabeth looked at her. 'It's true that you've all lived together for quite a few years.'

'I feel petrified,' Roslynn confessed. 'Oh, why did Sholto say they could come!'

'They're your relations, my dear,' Elizabeth pointed out dryly. 'Sholto feels we really can't keep them away.'

'They have a right to see me?'

'Something like that,' Elizabeth agreed after a curious hesitation. 'Anyway, you're looking so much better than when you arrived.'

'That's because of all the loving care.' Roslynn sighed and lay back on the sweet-smelling grass. 'Why is it I feel I've known you and Sholto for ever?'

'I have to admit I feel the same,' Elizabeth smiled. 'I suppose it's an awareness that we think and feel the same. For instance, it's doubling my pleasure to know I have a young person here with me to share my great love of my garden. It's also a very interesting idea of yours for me to write a book. If I say so myself, I've a lot of advice and a few valuable ideas to offer fellow gardeners. For instance, did you know I'm almost a world authority on camellias?'

'What an achievement! There must be hundreds of varieties here.'

'The perfect environment. I open the garden to the public for a few weeks in the spring. All the azaleas, rhododendrons and magnolias are out then. It's riotously beautiful. You have no idea.'

'I shall miss it when I'm not here.'

Because Elizabeth was moved, she looked away. 'I suppose you'd like lunch?'

'What time is it?' Roslynn asked lazily.

'Almost one.' Elizabeth glanced casually at her watch. 'Do you realise we've been sitting here talking for the best part of two hours?'

'It's been good.'

'You're a *nice* child,' Elizabeth said, knowing it went beyond niceness. Sholto's young patient she had found to be sensitive, considerate, well educated and beautifully mannered. She was also highly appreciative of anything that was done for her. Already Annie doted on her, thinking up all sorts of delicacies to tempt her to eat, something she was presently not interested in.

'Are you sure Sholto's going to stay the whole weekend?' Roslynn asked, not for the first time.

'He said he would,' Elizabeth nodded in her emphatic fashion. 'Be assured it's going to work out all right.'

'I can't think I was ever in love,' Roslynn said, reaching to stroke the petal of a rose just out of touch.

'But you *were* engaged,' Elizabeth reminded her gently.

'Then I can't understand how I'm no longer attracted to my fiancé.'

'He must find that very difficult to accept,' Elizabeth, always fair-minded, instantly replied.

'I guess I'm making a lot of people unhappy,' Roslynn sighed.

'I'm sure, Roslynn, they understand.'

'No.' Roslynn sat up, fingering the lush grass. She was dressed in yellow cotton pants and a yellow and white pinstriped cotton shirt and she looked as straight-legged and clean cut as a young boy, an illusion heightened by the extreme slightness of her figure and the closeness of the curling fronds of rose-bronze hair to her delicate skull. 'Kenneth doesn't believe in my amnesia,' she confided.

'So Sholto told me.'

'You're very close, aren't you?' said Roslynn, thinking how perfect that was.

'What can I say?' Elizabeth smiled. 'I could never wish for a finer grandson, or one I can love so whole-heartedly. I have other grandchildren, you know. Sholto's sisters all married prominent men, but Sholto always was my great favourite. Even as a child he inspired great love and confidence. We knew too that he was going to follow the family medical tradition, which is in many ways a hard life.'

'He's a very feeling man,' Roslynn agreed.

'And he suffers for it,' Elizabeth gave a serious smile. 'It's not always easy to keep one's shield up in the face of suffering.'

'No,' Roslynn returned poignantly. 'You used to practise too?'

'For many years,' said Elizabeth in her deep and certain tone. 'That was how I met my husband. He didn't greatly esteem women doctors at the time, but I soon changed his mind.'

'Sholto resembles him very closely,' Roslynn remarked, having studied at length the large portrait of Andrew McNaughton which hung above the mantelpiece in the library. 'The same startling blue-green eyes and the same clean bone structure, the way the taut flesh follows the bone.'

'I suspect you're a little in love with him,' said Elizabeth.

'Sad, isn't it?'

'And understandable to a great extent,' Elizabeth chuckled.

'He's only deeply concerned for me.'

'Of course,' Elizabeth agreed lightly. 'Now what about lunch? I expect Annie will be walking through that gate in a moment telling us she's made a quiche.'

'She's a particularly good cook.' Roslynn rose gracefully to her feet and held out her hand to the old lady.

'Which I'm sorry to tell you, I'm not. Never had the time. My greatest fear when I first married was that I was going to burn everything, which I did. Always had my head in a textbook. For a long time my poor Drew went chronically hungry.'

Together, companionably, they walked back to the house, where Annie appeared in the hallway to tell them lunch was ready.

Exactly at dusk on the Friday evening Sholto arrived with Roslynn's 'family'.

'I feel distinctly odd,' she told Elizabeth, who placed a calming hand on her arm. She was very pale under the faint gilding the summer sun had given her, small and delicate in a demure cream cotton dress with lace.

'You'll be fine.' In actual fact, Elizabeth too was nervous. Not of her visitors, she had entertained scores of visitors throughout her long life, but their effect on this young girl. Her physical condition was good but not great. No one could afford to ignore her mental condition.

Sholto, very tall and severely handsome, was

bringing them through the open doorway.

'Rosa!' The golden young man didn't wait for introductions but moved towards Roslynn at once, taking her unresisting young body into his arms and brushing her mouth with his own.

Speaking formally, Sholto introduced the woman, then the suddenly attentive young man to his grandmother, and somehow Roslynn managed to move closer to him as though she desperately needed his support. He had spoken to her only very briefly, just her name, his brilliant eyes resting in hers for only a heartbeat of time.

'*Roslynn*.' Now the woman stood before her, a smoother, older, even more golden version of the son. She put her hands out in a controlled gesture of affection, but Roslynn couldn't will herself to respond. 'Of course you know me?'

The blackness and frustration welled up in her. 'I want to.'

'My dear!' She was enveloped in a perfumed grasp, not daring to pull away. Something was swimming close to her, a certain panic, but the woman released her and Roslynn was free to stand alone.

'It's so kind of you, Mrs McNaughton, to invite us here.'

'Of course we would want to make it easy for you to see Roslynn,' Elizabeth McNaughton said, her patrician face impassive.

'It's Lady McNaughton,' Roslynn informed Kenneth a little tersely.

'I beg your pardon,' Vanessa Remington's fine brows darted together. 'I didn't know.'

'No matter,' Elizabeth McNaughton said easily. 'My late husband was knighted many years ago.'

While the visitors were being escorted to their rooms, Roslynn sank into an armchair in the drawing room.

'Nothing?' Sholto asked.

'Are you absolutely certain I'm Roslynn Ferrier?' she asked a little wildly.

'It won't help to become emotional, but I know anything else won't be easy.'

'I don't *know* her,' she whispered. 'And I don't want him to kiss me.'

'Difficult,' Sholto mused. 'Poor devil!'

'I swear I've never been engaged in my life.'

'You certainly hate the idea of it now. Anyway,' Sholto changed the subject deliberately, 'how are you? You look very much better.' His vivid eyes probed her face and her slight frame.

'I feel better,' she said. 'I really do. Elizabeth has been so kind to me—Annie and Bill too. Do you think I could stay here for ever?'

He seemed reluctant to answer, and she flushed at the impulsiveness of her tongue. 'I'm sorry, I'm embarrassing you.'

'You're not, Roslynn,' he said smoothly. 'You know perfectly well you're welcome to stay as long as you like. I can see my grandmother already regards you as family, the thing is you have a few urgent decisions to make. Mrs Remington has arrived, backed up by—Kenneth to take you home. Both of them have spoken to me of their deep concern for you.'

'You know perfectly well I don't *know* them, 'Roslynn interrupted with a pathetic little motion of her hands. 'Please don't send me back!'

'You don't have to go anywhere,' he said tersely, 'if you don't want to go. I've tried to explain your condition to Mrs Remington, but she assures me she's perfectly capable of getting you all the help you need.'

'I don't want her help,' said Roslynn, staring up at him. 'I can hardly accept let alone understand what has happened to me, but I *do* know how I feel now. I'm very much afraid my only relatives are now strangers to me.'

'You must see that they have difficulty accepting this themselves?'

'Of course,' she said miserably.

'Well, we won't consider anything now,' his penetrating glance slanted over her. 'You'll have the whole weekend to try and relate again. It's even a possibility that some memories will be stirred. After that, we'll have to consider the only possible courses of action. Neither Mrs Remington nor her son can stay on here indefinitely.'

'Actually Kenneth suggested we might take a house together,' she gave a strange little laugh.

'That's hardly what his mother intends to do,' Sholto pointed out with some irony. 'As soon as you're fit enough for the long flight, she would like to take you back to England.'

'And the odd thing is, I don't want to go. 'She looked up at his handsome, sombre face. 'I have, as the saying goes, suffered a reversal. I've forgotten my old life. I've left the past behind.'

Dinner was an uneasy meal, though Annie had prepared and served it with great care. They used the formal dining room for the first time, oak-panelled and able to accommodate a couple of dozen people if it had to, and against the dark wall and the array of gilt-framed paintings, Vanessa Remington's golden head stood up in stylish relief. It was clear too at a glance that Mrs Remington was a very handsome woman indeed and in particular, rather overpowering.

In contrast to her very fashionable elegance Elizabeth McNaughton wore a favourite blue silk dress she had had for years, and Roslynn looked like a child with her enormous eyes and her shorn head.

'I could never in all conscience go back without her.' Vanessa let her smiling glance rest on Sholto's darkened face. He was looking severely handsome with that remote expression he wore like a cloak.

'Yes, no doubt you feel like that,' he said quietly, 'but we must keep in mind what's best for Roslynn. Until she effectively regains her memory it might be best if she follows her own plans.'

'But you want to come back with us, don't you, darling?' Vanessa looked across the table at the silent girl. 'The house is waiting to welcome you back. You used to love it so. Roslynn,' she informed the others, 'is the proud owner of a very beautiful home, a Georgian residence our dear Charles bought when it was in a very run-down state and brought to magnificence.'

'Where exactly *is* it?' Sholto asked. 'I travelled very happily all over the U.K. in my student days. I know Sussex fairly well.'

Vanessa put her wine glass down and leaned forward, vigorously reeling off the names of places, landmarks, Sholto would have seen. She looked like a collector eagerly discussing the site of a treasure.

'Ah yes,' said Elizabeth, clearly getting in the picture too. 'You can't be very far away from the sea?'

'No, not at all. I only wish I had a photograph to show you. Such a lovely house, and though it long ago lost the thirty acres or so that used to be around it we still have a huge and splendid garden.'

'You're a keen gardener?' Elizabeth McNaughton asked with a considerable lightening of her rather formal expression.

'Nothing so physical or energetic,' Kenneth gave his mother an enigmatic smile. 'We have two gardeners, I'm told—one permanent, I recognise, and another fellow who comes and goes.'

'Charles arranged it all,' Vanessa told them. 'Of course he had a very good landscape architect to help him.'

'And my mother.' Roslynn had her slender fingers to her forehead. 'You must have known.' She frowned as though her head was hurting her.

'Roslynn darling!' Vanessa said anxiously.

'All right—we'll stay very quiet. 'Instantly Sholto assumed command. 'Has it happened again, Roslynn?'

'I'm sure I remember my mother. I *couldn't* forget her.'

'Look in the mirror if you want to remember her,' Kenneth supplied. 'You're absolutely the image of your mother—triangular face, same eyes and mouth, and that wonderful colouring.'

Vanessa was paying no attention to her son, staring at Roslynn's small face, ablaze with some emotion. 'I'm sure I could get your memory back for you in five minutes.'

'No, no, no,' Elizabeth said. 'She couldn't bear it.'

'My *dear* Lady McNaughton,' Vanessa protested, 'I don't really care for the implications of that remark.'

'I imagine you haven't been here long enough to know Roslynn is frightened,' Sholto pointed out.

'But how stupid!' Vanessa burst out. 'What could she possibly be frightened of?'

'*One*,' said Kenneth. . . .

'I think it would only make things worse for her to discuss it now,' Sholto said.

Vanessa stared at him, her anger barely concealed. 'Don't you think you're being over-protective, Doctor McNaughton? Let's get it over with now.'

'Indeed, *no*.' Quite easily he stared her down. 'Patience and understanding are called for now. Doors seem to be opening and closing momentarily in Roslynn's mind. Her whole memory could seize her at any time. I can't have her disturbed beyond a reasonable point. She is still my patient and I don't want to see too many drains on her physical strength.'

'Forgive me.' Immediately Vanessa looked contrite. 'I'm forever looking for short cuts—it's part of my nature. By the same token, Doctor McNaughton, I'm sure you realise Roslynn would make much faster progress in her own home. All the sights and sounds she would recognise. She would be able to see all her old friends and we have an excellent family doctor to keep her under close observation.'

'You're talking about me as though I were a child,' Roslynn protested. 'I may not have my memory, but I think I can look after myself. At least when I'm stronger.' She put out a hand and touched Lady McNaughton's. 'There must have been something I didn't like, something to make me run away. That's an inescapable aspect of the whole situation. I *did* run away. I did travel all the way to Australia. Why?'

A hot flush stained Vanessa's high cheekbones. 'We can't explain all that in a few moments, Roslynn. Only in as much as you were deeply disturbed by your sister's death.'

Roslynn thrust her chair back and stood up. 'Please excuse me.' Her heart was beating faster than her flying legs. She ran out of the dining room and straight up the stairway so that Sholto, coming after her, could see she was heading for her room.

With a few long swift strides he was up the stairs and after her, catching her up before she had even reached her door. 'Roslynn,' he said with an authority she couldn't reject.

'Oh, what's to *become* of me?' She collapsed against him, pounding her two fists against his chest. Her ears were roaring with a deluge of sounds. Screaming, cries. . . .

He looked down at her small, strained face. She was very pale. 'Come, try to get yourself together. You *can* do it. Show me.'

'I can't,' she said more quietly. 'I'm going insane.'

'No, what you feel is a terrible frustration. Your memory will return. All the signs are there, the flashes.'

'I can hear crying, screaming in my ears,' she said pathetically.

He was holding her very gently to calm her. 'I expect the memory of your own tears. You can't accept as yet the tragic loss of your sister. There were only the two of you and you must have been very close.'

'Yes,' she said in a shuddering breath.

'Are you feeling better?'

'I couldn't possibly go back to the dinner table. I don't like Mrs Remington.'

'You said yourself you're not a baby.' There was just the faintest trace of tenderness in his chiding tone. 'It's a very difficult position for her to be in too. Going on the bare facts, you once accepted her guardianship quite happily. You once cared enough about that young man to contemplate marrying him.'

'I must have been desperate.' It was perfect, just for a while, to rest against him and feed on his enormous strength.

'Not desperate—*different*. He insisted that you were very much in love.'

'Extraordinary, isn't it?' She lifted her head and stared into his eyes. His dark face was very composed, very controlled, except for the brilliantly alive eyes. So often Roslynn had been betrayed into thinking there was some special feeling for her in them. 'If you really think I should see Dr Pirelli, I will.'

He nodded, without releasing her. 'Especially if I can manage to get him up here. He doesn't need any special place to treat you and I really think you should stay here with Gran caring for you.'

'What about Mrs Remington?'

'I don't know exactly. *Yet*. She told me she'd counted on staying a month at the most.'

'She's only been here two days.'

'You don't want me to suggest she spend the time here? It's a very large house and Annie is excellent when it comes to catering for guests.'

'But *you* won't be here.' Without even thinking she linked her arms around his waist.

'I thought I told you,' Sholto said mildly.

'And I heard it with my head. It's just my arms that won't behave.' She looked up at him for a moment then dropped her arms to her side. 'What's wrong with appealing to you for support?'

'*You* know.' He laid his finger on the point of her chin. His eyes had changed colour now, more green than blue.

'I have absolutely no desire to fall in love with anyone.'

'Quite certain?' he asked her, a dry note in his voice.

'Almost. I mean, until I get my memory back.'

He groaned lightly. 'Okay, maybe we can drop the subject until then.'

Not surprisingly conversation was very stilted in the drawing room. Looking bewildered and upset, Kenneth jumped up from his chair and came towards them. 'How do you feel now, darling?'

'I'm sorry I ran away like that,' Roslynn apologised. 'I'm running a bit to hysteria these days.'

'Come and sit beside me,' Vanessa patted the
cushioned upholstery of a French settee. 'We've all
suffered a great shock, but I know we're going to
come to an agreement. All the time I was travelling
my one thought was to bring comfort. I like to think
I know something about it. Roslynn came to me
when she was only ten years old, and I took her to
my heart from the start.'

Feeling almost like a prisoner, Roslynn went to sit
beside the stunningly groomed woman she should be
calling 'Aunt'. The woman took her hand and held
it, and it cost Roslynn a real effort not to pull away.

Vanessa Remington looked down at their joined
hands and sighed deeply. 'It was a tremendous relief
to us to hear you'd been found, just as we were
terribly shocked to know of your accident. Such a
bad one—and your operation! I can only say again,
Dr McNaughton,' she turned to him, 'how deeply
grateful we are to you for your skill and your kindness. Naturally we'll take care of the bill.'

'Please——' Roslynn had reached the stage when
she just had to pull away, 'I'm sure I can attend to
all that myself, even as I'm sure Mr McNaughton
doesn't particularly care.'

'Would anyone care for more coffee?' Elizabeth
McNaughton asked smoothly as the colour rushed
up Vanessa's long, unlined neck.

'Thank you, yes.' Kenneth presented her with his
empty cup. 'I was wondering, Doctor, if Roslynn

might walk a little with me in the garden? It's such a beautiful night and we always used to talk everything over together, all our lives. Now everything's different, I suppose, temporarily, but I can still be quite a bit of help.'

'Why not ask *me*?' Roslynn suggested, not quietly. 'I might be a new person, but my age hasn't changed. I'm nineteen, not nine.'

'Of course you are, darling!' Kenneth gazed at her ardently, 'but Dr McNaughton has assured us you're a long way from full recovery.'

'Not my exact words,' Sholto remarked sardonically. 'But Roslynn will know best how she feels.'

Again Kenneth gave her that pleading look and she didn't know whether to sigh or scream aloud. How could she possibly find it—well, repulsive—to walk in the garden with this attentive, good-looking and even sweet-natured young man? His devotion to his mother was astonishing, though Roslynn thought it showed a trace of fear of going against such a determined woman. In the end, of course, she told him she would go, and a kind of triumph glittered in Vanessa's hazel eyes.

Outside under the flickering stars the air was like incense and Roslynn filled her lungs with it in a sudden burst of resilience. It was true she had made a remarkable recovery from major surgery of the most delicate and dangerous type, yet she was reasonably certain she couldn't withstand too many emotional shocks.

'Roslynn,' said Kenneth, and slipped his arm

around her, 'I've been desperate to get you to myself.'

'Oh, please, Kenneth,' she swung inwards to face him, 'I don't feel I can be burdened with emotional situations. Please try to understand.'

'But can't we talk?' He bent his blond head over her with the primeval instinct of possession. 'Surely it will help if we discuss your problems? It might be the first step towards solving them.'

'On the other hand, it might make things worse.' Her grey eyes were wide and troubled, but he could only catch their sparkle.

'Oh, *darling*!' He tried to kiss her mouth.

Instinctively she swung her head away and his kiss landed somewhere near her ear. 'I *will* make you admit it.' It was the simplest matter for him to cleave her fragile body to his own.

'If you don't let me go I'll scream,' she said in a voice of such purpose it amazed her. Her legs were trembling, why wasn't her voice?

'Little liar!'

She lifted her hand and slapped him, far from a vicious blow but one to make him jump back. 'I just can't understand you, Rosa, at all. Once you would have done anything for me, now you're trying to hurt me in any way you can.'

'I'm suffering too,' she exclaimed. 'You don't seem to believe in my amnesia, but believe me, it's very real. I can't conquer it no matter how hard I try. Sometimes I see things very dimly, but at the very moment I reach out to grasp it, it disappears.'

'Very well,' he said coldly, 'what do we do now?'

'You said you wanted to walk in the garden.'

'What I *want* to do, what *Mother* wants to do, is get you home. You're acting as if *we* are the strangers and these people are your friends.'

'I'm sorry,' she said quietly, 'but that's how I feel.'

'I know what's happened, of course,' he said tightly, 'you've got an outsize crush on McNaughton. It often happens, this doctor—patient relationship, but there's a quick cure. *Break it.*'

'First I want to feel a whole lot stronger.' She turned away slowly and walked towards a stone garden seat, conscious that he was following her, his eyes bent imploringly on her.

'You realise Mother can't wait around for ever?' He sat listlessly by her side. 'At the very most, we can only remain here a few weeks.'

'You don't have to remain here at all. I don't want to be deliberately cruel, but I've quite literally lost my past life. As soon as it comes back again, I have to make a few important decisions myself. One of them is where I'm going to live.'

'Why, surely at Lakeview?' He sounded very agitated.

'*Where?*' Something snapped in her mind.

'For God's sake, Rosa,' Kenneth exclaimed with the utmost frustration, 'the *house!*'

One moment she seemed to be sitting beside him on the old stone bench, the next sprawling on the grass.

'Oh!' Kenneth was down beside, her sounding as if he was about to cry. 'Lie quietly, darling, I'll get McNaughton.'

Roslynn tried to struggle up, but felt so weak she had to fall back, her physical condition plainly showing.

'Lakeview,' she said aloud, and her tremulous young voice sounded piteous in the night-time stillness.

They were back in a moment, Sholto dropping to his knees, remaining there for a moment for a quick check of her prone figure, then lifting her bodily into his arms, holding her like a sick and frightened child.

'My God, Kenneth, what happened?' Vanessa's voice rose sharp and accusing.

'*Nothing!*' Kenneth was struggling with his own fears. 'One moment we were talking, then the next she pitched forward on to the grass. I couldn't believe it.'

'Roslynn, can you hear me?' Vanessa demanded.

'There is something you'll all have to do,' Sholto ordered, 'that is keep quiet and keep calm. We all want to help Roslynn.'

Mother and son trooped after him into the house, where Elizabeth met them with a face full of concern but mercifully no questions. 'I'll take her to her room,' Sholto said.

'I'll come up with you,' said Vanessa, her elegant face quite pale.

'Go to hell,' Roslynn whispered helplessly, but Sholto heard her. His dark face closed right up and the muscles stood out along his taut jawline.

'It might be best, Mrs Remington, if you allow me to handle this. It's obvious Roslynn is greatly disturbed.'

'Very well.' Forceful as she was, Vanessa did not
dare to challenge him.

'Thank you.' His vibrant voice sounded harsh.
'Gran, I believe our guests could do with some
brandy.'

'Please,' Kenneth agreed, and laughed shortly. 'I
think I must sit down, if you don't mind.'

'My dear boy!' All Elizabeth McNaughton's professional qualities surfaced at once. 'Come back into
the drawing room. You too, Mrs Remington. I can
see you're shaken.'

In the mellow beauty of the big bedroom very
little could be done for Roslynn except put her out.
Her excitement, agitation, was extravagant and
under the circumstances very bad for her. She seemed
only half aware of what she was saying, the words
tumbling out, the cries and accusations.

A crisis had been precipitated, and Sholto watched
her face uneasily until she lapsed into unconsciousness, her too slender body ceasing its thrashing
and curling into a relaxed state.

'What's happened, Sholto?' Nothing could have
kept Elizabeth McNaughton away from that
room.

'I would say she has her memory back, and most
painfully,' he said after a few moments.

'Whatever brought it on?' Elizabeth approached
the bed, staring down at the unconscious girl. She
looked heartbreakingly young and defenceless, the
brightly coloured flames of hair sleekly following the
outline of her delicate skull. 'Oh dear, Sholto, she
does look so vulnerable.'

'Too vulnerable,' he said grimly. 'I wonder if she can take it.'

'I'm greatly concerned about the Remingtons as well,' Elizabeth answered him. 'They're very much upset.'

'I can believe it,' Sholto put out a long, beautifully made hand and stroked Roslynn's temple. 'She's obviously riddled with guilt.'

'*That* child?' Elizabeth's fine dark eyes flew to his stark face. 'Whatever could *she* have done to make her feel guilty?'

'When she was enjoying herself her sister was drowning. She *had* to forget it, at least for a time.'

'Oh, Sholto!' The old lady leaned against the four-poster for support.

Behind them there was a knock on the door and as they turned around they were confronted by Vanessa and a very aghast-looking son. 'Forgive me, but I couldn't stay away.'

'Come in for a moment,' said Sholto, almost but not quite gently. 'I've had to put her out.'

'She's remembered?' Kenneth asked, a sick tint to his smooth skin.

'Almost certainly.' Sholto looked across at him broodingly. 'What exactly did you say the moment before she fainted?'

'Why, nothing.'

'*Kenneth!*' his mother said sharply. 'Think hard.'

'She was talking about where she was going to live and I said surely nowhere else but Lakeview.'

'And that did it?' Vanessa gasped.

'I take it Lakeview is the name of your home?'

'Why, of course!' Vanessa answered him, her golden hair glowing in the subdued light. 'Why should *that* hurt her? She loved the place as none of us did except perhaps me.'

'And there's a lake on the property?'

'Not very far away. A most beautiful place.'

'And the scene of her sister's drowning.' It wasn't a question, but a statement.

'The most terrible tragedy.' Vanessa bent her head with a genuine stab of pain. 'None of us have ever been able to believe it. Normally Marianne was the most sensible girl in the world, but she did have her moments when she railed at her general frailty. She had rheumatic fever as a child and it left her with a weakened heart. Nothing very serious, but she always had to take care.' Vanessa spoke as though her mind was many thousands of miles away. 'Marianne was never an easy girl. One couldn't enjoy her like Roslynn, who was always a delightful child. As she got older Marianne was always very anxious to put us down, put us in our place. Of course Lakeview belonged to the girls, but I came to regard it as my own home. And it would have been with Roslynn. She has a very generous, appreciative nature. Marianne was quite different, or her delicate health obviously affected her. Things came to a head, I suppose, after Roslynn and Kenneth became engaged. Marianne was very much against it.'

'She considered her sister too young?'

'Roslynn always knew her own mind,' Kenneth answered Sholto's question. 'If you can believe it, I always thought Marianne was a little in love with me. Naturally I never said anything about it to either of the girls. Certainly not Roslynn. She would have renounced anything her sister wanted. She adored her sister and always felt guilty that she was the one who got all the love. It just happened naturally. People took to Roslynn where they always had reservations about Marianne.'

All the time he was listening Sholto's chiselled mouth looked hard and set. 'Did no one realise on that particular day that Marianne was in difficulties?'

'No, never! As if anyone could!' Kenneth exclaimed.

'Roslynn apparently believes *you* acted too late.'

'My God!' Vanessa collapsed into a chair, her face terrible. 'We know of Roslynn's suspicions, Doctor, but they were part of her own feelings of guilt. It was a sick, twisted feeling. I know my son. What Roslynn believes is unthinkable.'

'Sadly, it will take therapy to help her,' Sholto said.

'Certainly. These feelings have to be brought out into the open.' Vanessa stared back at him, once more in full control. 'Roslynn has been acting under excessive strain. Even before her accident. For instance, she ran away—we thought to her friends in the south of France. Marianne's tragic death destroyed something precious between us all. Nothing in this world gave me more pleasure than when Roslynn and Kenneth came to me telling me they wanted to get engaged. It seemed like the perfect solution to everything.'

'You're tired, Mrs Remington,' Elizabeth interrupted.

'Deadly tired, now,' Vanessa agreed.

'Then, as it's almost midnight, we should all retire. Problems, anxieties seem so much worse when one is tired.'

'I daresay.'

Kenneth lent his mother a supportive hand, his hazel eyes shying away from the doctor's. 'I'll say goodnight as well. In spite of everything, the way Roslynn has acted, the things she has even allowed herself to think, I still love her. I'll always love her.'

'Then may I suggest,' Sholto said tellingly, 'you give her time.'

CHAPTER FIVE

ABOUT three o'clock in the morning Roslynn came to with a cry that seemed to fill her throat with thunder but was only a frenzied moan.

'Quiet, Roslynn, I'm here.' A familiar voice soothed her, cool fingers on her pulse.

She sighed jaggedly, too spent to speak. The truth had returned to her, too terrible to deny. On the bedside table beneath the lamp and a bowl of roses a little French porcelain clock chimed the hours.

Sholto too gave vent to a faint sigh. 'You should have slept through.'

For answer she just stared at him, the shock of

waking alleviated by his presence. He was still wearing the clothes he had worn at dinner minus his jacket and tie, and she let her eyes wander over his tall frame, the sombre face that was too full of understanding to be imperious, though the power was there, impossible for him to give up.

'I've been dreaming,' she said. 'Bad dreams, always the same.'

'You've been crying as well.' His fingertip on her cheekbones was exquisitely gentle. 'Try to hold yourself together inside. I know how you feel.'

'Then you're the only one!' She looked intensely into his brilliant eyes. What made them so brilliant? Their colour was extraordinary. 'I'm glad you're here.' His presence was the greatest security she had ever known.

'Can you talk to me?' He sat down on the side of the bed and took her hand.

'I'm sure you don't want to hear,' she said tragically.

'I do.' His eyes were so clear, blue-green like the sea.

Her mouth parted on words, but no sounds came out. Her eyes filled with tears and she pressed her face into the pillows.

'*Roslynn.*'

She turned back her head. She had to tell him or go mad. She didn't realise it, but she was holding on to his hand for dear life.

'Easy, little one,' he soothed. '*Easy.*'

'Just one word, and I *knew*. I remembered.'

'Yes.'

'I think I love you,' she said wonderingly.

It made him smile. 'No, Roslynn. Love is something else. You trust me.'

'Whatever,' she said in a low voice, 'I know I can tell you anything. Even when it's very bad.'

'So?'

But then she seized up and he put his hand on her shoulder. Something that was so dangerous because it made her feel so differently, made her body react in a way she could never put into words. He didn't like it. He probably couldn't bear women falling in love with him. She turned her head so that her cheek grazed his hand. 'Marianne never liked Kenneth,' she told him, 'but I didn't know. I mean, Marianne never spoke to me about the deficiencies in Kenneth's character. I suppose she thought I would come to see them myself, but I didn't until they were showing through pretty badly. Aunt Vanessa is the strong one. Jeremy and Kip just do what they're told.'

'Tell me about Marianne.'

'I can't,' she said. 'I'll cry.'

'It's better to be *able* to cry, little one.'

'She was my sister,' Roslynn said simply. 'My big sister. The one I looked to when we didn't have anyone in the world.'

'You had your Aunt Vanessa.'

'One can't force love,' she said. 'I've always been very grateful to Aunt Vanessa and in many ways she was very good to us, but she doesn't really have a lovable personality. She's too certain she's always right, and in certain moods she can be very spiteful.'

'Marianne didn't like her either?'

'Marianne was of an age when she missed our

mother dreadfully. I did too, but I was the one who cried a lot. Marianne stayed very withdrawn and quiet, nursing her grief. I suppose in a way she always resented Aunt Vanessa. Perhaps she would have resented any woman, but particularly Aunt Vanessa with her kind of personality. I'm quite sure Marianne could never have held out against a woman like Elizabeth, for example. But Aunt Vanessa was never like that. She's a person who always likes to be doing things *herself*. She revelled in living a . . . a . . . a . . . at. . . .'

'Lakeview,' he said, to overcome that difficult little stammer.

'Yet nothing really happened until Kip and I decided to get engaged.'

'You loved him?' He sought her eyes and held them.

'I . . . I *thought* I did. He was such fun, and I sort of grew up with that sort of thing in my mind. Afterwards Marianne told me it had been planted very early, but she was going to insist I had time.'

'Until you were twenty-one.'

'How did you know?'

'It seems a reasonable age.'

'From the night of the party on there were arguments,' she said, and her fingernails bit into the palm of his hand. 'Marianne wasn't very strong physically, but she was very strong inside. Like Daddy. I always thought she had the wonderful solidity I lacked. I've always been impulsive, a too spontaneous sort of person. Marianne used to call it outgoing because she especially loved me. She never wanted me to marry Kenneth and really I don't think I would have, even with the crushing weight of Aunt Vanessa's approval. I'm not entirely a fool.'

'Only very young,' Sholto said conclusively.

'Aunt Vanessa seemed to think she would always live at . . . home.'

'That would have been awkward, surely, after you were married?'

'It's possible Aunt Vanessa thought I would always remain a child while she continued to hold court.'

'And Kenneth didn't understand this?'

'I don't think Kip ever had too many ideas of his own. Both he and Jeremy have always lived in Aunt Vanessa's shadow. She outshone them both in looks and brains and ambitions, though Marianne once claimed they were all parasites. She was very angry at the time and I told her she was exaggerating. How I wish I hadn't! She was quite right.'

Her forehead was quite damp and he smoothed back the tiny, dark red curls, his face in deep shadow. 'Can you tell me about that terrible day?'

Roslynn seemed to shiver slightly, though it was a warm night. 'I think so,' she said unsteadily, echoes of the old screaming tearing through her head. 'It was a hot day, one of those hot days out of nowhere, and a few of us decided on a picnic at the lake.' Now her heart was racing, the beat hurting her.

'Tell me.'

Her eyes fixed themselves on his face so imploringly that Sholto acted quite instinctively, picking her up out of the bed and carrying her to one of the deeply upholstered armchairs where he lowered himself into it with her cradled in his lap.

'Why do you want to hear?' Her two arms encircled his neck, though she kept her head hidden against his chest.

'It's important, Roslynn, for you to tell me exactly what happened.'

'At first Marianne wouldn't go in—she said the water was too cold. But it wasn't, it was glorious. I was the one who persuaded her.'

'A swim wouldn't have hurt her,' he said quietly.

'It was at least an hour after our lunch. Marianne made us all wait. She was always the sensible one.' She was quiet for a moment listening to his heart. Such a strong, steady beat, while hers seemed to be flickering wildly.

'Marianne had had rheumatic fever?'

'Yes.'

He barely heard her little whisper, it was so quiet.

'She was always under a doctor?'

'Yes. Aunt Vanessa made sure she always had the best of care. She wasn't an invalid, you understand, or anything like it—she simply had to be more careful than was usual. Doctor Ellis used to encourage her to take lots of walks, swim if she wanted to. She just had to remember not to get overtired. We were all very protective of her—all of us, including Kip, though they never did get on. Kip used to say Marianne was jealous, but I know now she was just worried.'

Sholto tipped her head right back against his shoulder and looked at her. 'Did you all stay in the water longer than you intended?'

'I don't *know*,' she said desperately. 'I can swim like a fish.'

'Marianne swam quite well?'

'Of course. Daddy taught us almost before we could walk.' She took a deep breath and closed her eyes.

'You won't fall or faint,' he said impassively. 'I'm here. I'm holding you. Why don't you open your eyes?'

There was tremendous tension in her slight body, all but visible through the thinness of her palest apricot crêpe-de-chine nightdress. One thin strip was off her shoulder and her delicate breasts were framed by the deep V of lace. With a man's eyes Sholto saw that she was exquisitely formed, but it was a doctor's nature that was uppermost because he willed it that way, the tight control he held on himself making his handsome face formidable.

'You *are* going to tell me, Roslynn.'

A pulse was hammering away at the base of her tender young throat. She had the appearance of utter abandonment, beautiful and tragic. 'You weren't watching closely. . . .' Gravely he gave her a lead.

'No.' She whispered the word and burst out crying, her body very young and soft in his arms.

He tucked her head beneath his chin and let her cry, though her mouth was moving against his bare throat. He had never heard such sounds of desolation, and he had heard a great deal. His shirt was wet with her tears, but after a while he stopped her in case she made herself ill.

Very slowly he angled a box of pink tissues towards him and began drying her tears, with Roslynn so wrapped in misery she was oblivious to her déshabille, the fact that she was almost half naked in his arms.

'I'm sure Kip *knew*,' she whispered with intensity.

'What you're saying is very serious, Roslynn. You can't speak unless you're absolutely sure.'

'I feel it,' she insisted. 'I know Kip.' She began to cry again but soundlessly. 'I think for a moment he hesitated and then when he came to himself it was too late.'

'Roslynn, Roslynn,' he sighed.

'It was the way he denied it,' she said wildly, and he held her more tightly. 'I think he realised something was wrong, but something stopped him from acting at once.'

'But he *did* act?'

'Oh yes,' she said shudderingly. 'It was Kip who dived over and over again until we were all afraid something would happen to him as well. Afterwards I turned on him—attacked him.' In her agitation she even pounded his chest.

'So at the most all you have is a doubt?'

'I can never forget he hesitated.'

'You didn't see that, Roslynn, with your own eyes.'

She turned her head despairingly on his shoulder. 'I tell you I *know* Kip, as your grandmother knows you. I know the silly things he does in moments of stress.'

'But this is terrible, what you're saying. You should consider he had a moment's lapse. Perhaps he panicked. People react differently to alarm. Some race to the scene, others are driven to run for help. You said yourself he put himself in danger.'

'That was after,' she said with extreme bitterness.

'There was an inquest?'

'Yes. Death by misadventure.'

'I'm sure that young man has suffered torture.'

'He should,' she said intensely.

'So you ran away?'

'One day he might have turned his back on me as easily as he did on Marianne.'

'What you're accusing him of, Roslynn,' he said severely, 'is murder.'

'No,' she shook her head sadly. 'Truly—not murder but a moment of terrible, human weakness. Marianne was doing everything possible to break us up. Maybe Kip feared she would.'

She wasn't as distraught now as she had been, frowning as she adjusted the thin strap of her nightgown on her shoulder, a delicate flush rising to her cheeks. 'After this is all over, you'll never want to see me again.'

'Oh?' Sholto's smile became taut. 'What will you do about Remington? You have no concrete evidence against him, only a feeling. Feelings are no use in the courts, and you could be quite wrong. I must, in all justice, bring that to your mind. A man is not guilty of a crime because he's slow to act.'

'Surely he'd feel guilty in his own mind. *I* did.'

'*Why?*' His eyes that had been narrowed, suddenly blazed at her.

'Because of what I did. Getting engaged.' Her small face looked pinched. 'If we hadn't become engaged Marianne and Kip wouldn't finally have become enemies.'

'We can never forget Marianne's heart wasn't

strong,' said Sholto. 'That *is* true. I've made enquiries, Roslynn.'

'She didn't have a heart attack.'

'Her heart could have gone into spasm.'

Shattered, Roslynn huddled her head. 'Don't tell me you're taking Kip's part against me?'

'I'm trying to get at the truth,' he said, holding her tightly because she was trembling uncontrollably. 'For both your sakes, Roslynn. Your cousin too is very young. It's easy to show a weakness at twenty-two.'

'A weakness,' she murmured, 'but what was his motive? All I know is, now he frightens me. I pity him and despise him as well.'

'He knows,' said Sholto.

'Vanessa too sensed something was terribly wrong. No matter what else Vanessa is, she's physically brave.'

'Aren't we talking about morality?' he pointed out gently. 'We could discuss this for ever, Roslynn, and we'd never come closer to the truth. Only your cousin knows his immediate reactions, and he denies your terrible charge.'

'I'll never forgive him,' she said. '*Never*. I'll never forgive myself.'

'And all your old feeling for him?'

'It's gone,' she said sternly. 'Gone with Marianne.'

'And what if he's innocent?'

'He did this,' she said, shaking her head a little dazedly. 'Is it true I'm sitting in your lap?' She looked down contemplating the flimsiness of her pretty nightdress.

'I thought it might make it easier for you to endure.'

'You must find me pathetic,' she said brokenly.

'On the contrary, I think you have great strength.'

'Really?' She looked up at him steadily, over-powered by her complex feeling for him. 'I'm sure you didn't know I'd turn out to be a burden.'

'I knew you would turn out to play a more than ordinary role in my life.'

Without her volition her eyes dropped to his mouth. It was a mouth that betrayed him in a way because it was the mouth of a man of temperament, a man of strong passions.

'Perhaps I'd better tuck you up in bed,' he said, not really allowing himself to look at her.

'Oh, don't worry,' she murmured in confusion, the colour flooding her skin. 'You're such a responsible person.'

'Of course.' He lifted himself out of the chair with Roslynn in his arms quite easily. 'Do you feel easier?'

'Yes,' she said quietly. 'Does Aunt Vanessa know I know the whole truth?'

'None of us was exactly sure.' He put her down gently and she sank back on the pillows.

'What am I going to do now?' Her smoky eyes, faintly tilted at the corners, were full of uncertainty.

'Start to forgive yourself,' Sholto said immediately. 'You were in no way to blame for your sister's death, just as I can't blame myself when one of my patients dies on me. All we *can* do is our very best. A fatalist would tell you the exact hour of death is inescapable no matter what we do.'

'I don't think I can ever forgive Kip. God forgive me if I'm wrong, but I have the certain intuition he realised Marianne was in difficulties. It's the shadow on my life, the kind of knowledge that made my mind go blank.'

'Not *knowledge*, Roslynn,' he pointed out, 'a doubt based on our imperfect intuitions. You can't condemn him without a fair trial.'

'Then speak to him yourself,' she urged him, clutching at his sleeve. 'You have great experience of people's minds.'

'I'm a neurosurgeon, Roslynn. I deal in the diseases and disorders of the nervous system, not the psyche.'

'You're a very clever man,' she persisted. 'A highly trained observer and I've come to depend on you.' Utterly, she thought, but couldn't say aloud.

'Have you considered your cousin mightn't admit such a moment, even to himself? The mind throws up all sorts of barriers to conceal guilt. The boy's mother would be the best person to discover the truth.'

'She doesn't want to know,' Roslynn said wearily, her eyelids growing unaccountably heavy. 'Could you blame her?'

'I think you should sleep now,' he said with authority. 'There's nothing to be gained by overtaxing your strength.'

'I wish you'd stay here with me,' she said faintly, 'but that's selfish. You must be very tired.'

'Actually I'm not.' Sholto settled back in his chair.

'Close your eyes, Roslynn. I'll stay here until you're safely asleep.'

She awoke late in the morning, terribly lethargic in mind and body. From total darkness she had been pitchforked into complete remembrance of her whole life. It brought her no pleasure but a constant pain she would have to struggle to endure. She lay there for a moment staring up at the plastered ceiling which had been decorated with acorns and oak leaves. The cornice too was exquisite, the work of Italian crafts-men and hand-moulded on the premises. The cornice of her bedroom at Lakeview was based on the acan-thus leaf and the Tudor rose. She closed her eyes again with a sense of utter unreality, unwilling and unable to come to terms with what she must do.

'That's great!' smiled Annie, when she saw she was awake. 'I've got your breakfast, love.'

'You're too good to me, Annie.'

'I haven't put a pound on you, I see,' Annie answered.

'Give you time,' Roslynn smiled, and Annie set the tray down across her knees.

'Eat up every scrap.'

'Even a rose,' Roslynn sighed. 'What did I ever do to deserve such kindness?'

'Go on, you're easy to spoil,' Annie told her. 'When you're feeling a lot better I'm going to make you a really glamorous breakfast, not fruit and a boiled egg.'

'Lovely!' Annie's plump, tender-hearted face was so expectant Roslynn could do little else but smile. She lifted the pink rosebud to her nose, savouring the lovely scent. 'Everyone else up?' she asked, feigning lightness.

'The family had breakfast early, but I've only just cleared away after our guests. Lady McNaughton tells me you've regained your memory. Bill and I are so happy for you. It just had to come back.'

'Yes, Annie.' Roslynn picked up her grapefruit juice and drank it. There was no sense in ruining Annie's day by sighing.

Later she took a quick shower and dressed in her uniform of cotton slacks and tiny camisole top. Making decisions demanded stamina, but she felt as weak as a kitten.

'*Roslynn!*'

Aunt Vanessa had found her, nothing less than immaculate in a silk shirt and linen skirt, but there was a kind of pallor under her porcelain skin and the hazel eyes looked glazed from lack of sleep.

'Good morning, Aunt Vanessa.' Roslynn turned towards her.

'May we talk, Roslynn?'

'I don't see why not.'

Neither woman smiled and Roslynn watched while Vanessa seated herself then she too slid into a chair.

'I've never been faced with such an odd situation in my life,' Vanessa confided. 'Doctor McNaughton has had quite a talk to me this morning.'

'Oh?' Roslynn managed to look interested.

'This isn't easy for me, Roslynn,' Vanessa pointed out, rather flushed. 'Kenneth seems to think your . . . amnesia was all an elaborate piece of theatre.'

'And what do *you* think?'

'Frankly, I've never believed in amnesia myself.'

'Really?' Roslynn looked away over the terraced gardens. 'It's quite well documented.'

'At any rate,' Vanessa said dryly, 'the mists have apparently cleared.'

'Would that I were happier about that,' Roslynn returned meaningfully. 'I think we all had it as family when I decided to go away.'

'You're not *still* at it?' Vanessa pleaded raggedly. 'Surely we've all suffered enough? The whole business has been a nightmare.'

'Not a nightmare,' said Roslynn. 'It's real.'

'You can't mean it, Roslynn,' Vanessa cried out. 'Haven't you injured Kip enough? He *loves* you. He hasn't changed.'

'Have you ever asked him about that terrible day?' said Roslynn, and her voice shook with pain.

Vanessa lifted her white slender fingers and pressed them against her eyes. 'God, I'm tired,' she murmured.

'Will you answer me, Aunt Vanessa?' Roslynn's grey eyes glittered with strong feeling. 'You know Kip better than anyone.'

'I should think so,' Vanessa flashed at her. 'Let us not forget I'm his mother.'

'You haven't had any peace either,' Roslynn said.

In front of her eyes Vanessa seemed to age ten years. She put out a strong hand and clasped Roslynn's wrist. 'I swear to you, Roslynn, Kip is incapable of a wicked action. He might be stronger, I'll allow you, more positive, more clever, more ambitious, but by nature he's entirely non-aggressive.

Your judgments are terribly wrong. You used to be so sweet and so kind, but now you're almost as stern as poor Marianne.'

At the sound of her sister's name, Roslynn's eyes filled with tears. 'If you care for me at all, Aunt Vanessa,' she said quietly, 'don't malign my sister.'

'But, dearest girl!' Vanessa looked aghast. 'I'm only being truthful. *You're* accusing *my* son of something terrible, after all. You haven't even kept it secret from Dr McNaughton. How do we know he won't talk? I can't have Kenneth subjected to vicious rumours!'

'Better let it all drop,' said Roslynn said with a harshness in her clear voice. 'I'm very grateful to you, Aunt Vanessa, for all that you've done, but I'm not coming back to England with you—at least not for a while.'

'But what are you going to *do*?' Vanessa challenged her relentlessly. 'I mean, you can't stay here. I'm sure the McNaughtons are being very kind to you, but they'll want to settle back into their own routine. You can't allow yourself to impose on them.'

'I won't,' Roslynn said briskly, though her eyes were still shimmering with tears. 'As I almost stupidly forgot, I'm rich by ordinary standards. I can very easily find a place of my own.'

'But what about Lakeview?' Vanessa asked vigorously. 'How could you possibly find anywhere more beautiful than that? Why, do you realise you and Kip were to be married by Christmas?'

'No,' Roslynn shook her head, 'I think not. Even without Marianne's influence I don't believe I would have married Kip. I see now that what I felt for him was a great fondness, and you must remember you did everything you could to bring us together. Remember Peter Ward? His sister told me how you'd warned him off. Somehow I think you warned quite a few off: No use looking at Roslynn, she's for my son.'

'I'm quite sure it would have worked,' Vanessa said. 'I'm still sure. With a little help you'll regain some sense of proportion. Now, why don't we, when you're feeling a little stronger, do some travelling and enjoy it? At your age you should be full of joy, not clinging to old tragedies. I've been doing some thinking since Dr McNaughton spoke to me. You've always been volatile, highly strung, and if you'll forgive my saying so, darling, rather stubborn at times. I can't compel you to come back with me, but I do think I can compel some affection. We care for you—Jeremy, myself, and above all, Kip. Let us help you regain your balance. We'll take it very slowly with gentleness on both sides.

I can't, Roslynn thought, and I won't.

The weekend wore on interminably with neither side giving an inch. On the surface all was civilised, but underneath emotions raged savagely. All Roslynn longed for was peace, a time of solitude when she could begin to cope with the future, but Vanessa didn't intend for her to escape.

'She's an enormously determined woman,' Elizabeth told her grandson in private. 'It's rather neat really, the way Roslynn is evading her.'

'She has a great deal of courage,' Sholto agreed.

With communication so difficult even Vanessa didn't really want to stay on. Always a woman of action, she wanted to sweep Roslynn off, resolutely resisting the girl's wishes and return her to her own home, where if she had to she would lock her up until she came to her senses. When everything had once been so perfect, Vanessa began to consider the loss of Lakeview which she loved obsessively.

Finally Kenneth put in his impassioned plea.

'Rosa, underneath, I know you really love me.'

They were walking along the hillside planted with thousands of wildflowers winding their way down the slopes. It was another beautiful day of brilliant sunlight and cool shade, and Roslynn was bemoaning again how little she was seeing of Sholto. Though he was lavishing care on her he was keeping himself remote, perhaps dreading that she would blurt out that she was in love with him again. How could she have told him in the first place? It alarmed her even as she knew he could prompt her into telling him again. Such was the unreality of it all, she thought, and sighed.

'Rosa, are you listening?' Kenneth peered frustratedly into her face.

'Is it a kindness to keep pestering me?' she sighed.

'I'm being as gentle with you as I can.' He slipped his arm through hers and held her to his side. 'Oh, darling, admit it, *say* it.'

'I don't love you, Kip,' she said slowly.

'It's all Marianne's fault!' he shouted, his voice filled with anger. 'Fancy Marianne still affecting us now—she's *dead*!'

'And you stood there watching, didn't you?' Roslynn accused him with a terrible stillness.

The horror of it sobered Kenneth in an instant. 'You're mad, Ros,' he said with equal quietness. 'I might have been angry with Marianne and the way she was trying to come between us, but I could never destroy her. I dived for her a dozen times—you know that. It was a terrible accident, one that has preyed on your mind. You and Marianne were closer than most sisters. In a way she was always a little mother to you. That's why she resented Vanessa so much. She wanted to be your protector, your mentor, the one who told you who to marry.'

Roslynn stepped back and stared up at the cobalt sky. 'You paint a picture of Marianne that simply isn't true.'

'Everyone has many faces. Even you.'

'Go away, Kip,' she said hopelessly. 'Leave me alone.'

When he was a distance off Roslynn continued down the hill, trying to relax her jangled nerves. Her fear was that if she went back to the house Vanessa would immediately start on her, so she intended to walk until she ran out of physical and mental energy. If she was accusing Kenneth wrongly it was a grievous sin, but something very odd had certainly happened to Kenneth that day. A moment's aberration. Would anyone ever really know?

The sky was a magnificent, uniform blue with millions of golden lights flickering through the tops of the trees. Life had no solutions. One just had to keep on going. The grass swished around her bare ankles, an iridescent green, and she took care not to tread on the radiant little wildflowers that seemed to flower right down to the valley and beyond. Their sweetness threw up in the summer heat so that as she filled her lungs with their gentle fragrance; it brought solace to her sorrowful heart. Marianne had gone and she was the one who was left.

She walked as long as she could, more than was wise, for when she sank down in the dappled shade of a sweet gum her temples were dewed with sweat. She put up a hand limply and brushed it away. From somewhere high above her a magpie warbled happily, its notes as clear as a bell. It was even melodic if one had ears to hear.

An acute drowsiness seized her and she lay back in the luxuriant ground cover that grew even in shadow. Her arms were thrown back above her head and her rose-leaf crowned head turned wearily to the side. Would to God Aunt Vanessa and Kenneth would go away and stay away until such time she could look on them with a quiet heart. If she ever lived so long!

CHAPTER SIX

AN hour and more later Sholto saw the flash of her yellow dress through the dense woodland, and he had to stop a moment to cool his temper and a wealth of nagging anxieties. He had been calling for ten minutes, his voice echoing down the hillside, yet there she lay with her arms thrown up above her head in supplication to the sky. The drowsy heat of early afternoon was over and there was a thunderstorm threatening, the brilliant blue sky now banked up with dark clouds. What unnerved him above everything else was the way Remington had set him on the wrong path. He couldn't understand his motive. Surely the greater part of love was the care for the wellbeing of the beloved? He realised the boy was jealous, but Roslynn was alone on the hillside with a sky that was ready to unleash lightning and heavy rain.

'*Roslynn!*' A single glance told him she was merely sleeping, her head and her body curved towards him. She was breathing deeply and quietly, as tranquil as a child. It seemed a great pity to wake her, but they would have to run before the storm or take shelter in the old summerhouse halfway up the slope. He slid his arm under her and she gave a little inarticulate cry, but didn't open her eyes.

Exhausted, he thought. Striving to put distance between herself and her relations. 'Roslynn,' he said again, and put a little pressure beneath her ear, rousing her from her deep sleep.

Her eyes when they opened reflected no fear but gave him back a mirror image of himself. 'I was looking for you,' he said gently. 'There's going to be a storm.'

'Surely not?' Her breath rippled out on a contented sigh. He was here at last.

'Look above your head.'

'I don't want to look past you.' Her eyes were large and very soft.

Leaves scattered on the sudden wind and there was the wondrous heavy smell of an approaching storm. Roslynn realised now that she had been asleep for some time, but at least she had the joy of sharing a little of Sholto's time. She lifted her arms to him like outstretched wings and he lifted her in one graceful swoop, holding her in his strong arms.

'We *might* be able to make it back to the house.' he said dubiously.

'Why don't we just stay here and get soaked?'

'Because, young lady, you clearly need looking after.' His eyes were vivid in his dark, stupendous face.

'All right, then, I can run along beside you.'

'I think you've reached the end of your endurance,' he pointed out dryly. 'That was some sleep.'

'Well, carrying me is an ordeal.'

'Is it?' For answer he began to run with the first drops of rain falling, as tangy as lemons.

It was *glorious*! Roslynn felt like a lady with her knight, secure in his strength yet excited by his manhood.

It was a challenge to reach the summerhouse in time, but they did it just as the rain fell down in a silver curtain.

'Marvellous!' she said, standing against him, hearing the strong thud of his heart. 'I shall remember my doctor who can run uphill with a girl in his arms.'

'Don't you mean a wood nymph?' Sholto brushed a hand over her damp head where feathery curls clustered in tendrils.

Undreamed-of emotions soared in her, yet she went very still beneath his hand, as after a moment he did, both of them caught in a frieze.

They might have stayed that way, only thunder cracked along the great bowl of the sky and Sholto turned and pulled the shuttered door. 'The temperature has dropped. Pull those cushions around you.'

'I'm not cold.' How could she be, with fire galloping along her veins?

'It should be over quite soon. Storms are always like this in summer, short and spectacular.' He had his back to her looking out and she could see the beautiful shape of his head, the wideness of his shoulders and the elegant long lines of his body. She laid her face against a plump cushion, sapphire blue patterned with white flowers, desperately willing herself to act sensibly. She seemed to have so little armour against him, testing his control when he was bound to a line of action. Probably he wouldn't turn and look at her again until it was time to scale the rest of the distance to the house.

'Do you think Aunt Vanessa and Kip will go home?' she asked uncomfortably, aware of his and Elizabeth's great patience.

'They will if anyone answers my prayers,' he returned sardonically.

'You've been very courteous to them. I'm grateful.' In fact he had torn strips off Kenneth, who had crumbled in a way that stirred his anger and pity.

'I didn't think we'd get *one* moment to talk together.'

She sounded so plaintive he had to smile. 'It's a very complex situation, isn't it, Roslynn?'

She bit her lip. 'I don't think I can ever go back to my old life.' The rain was drumming harder now, maintaining a steady roar, so she got up and crossed to where he was standing.

'You can't take on too much now.'

'Is that a warning?' She lifted her head and stared at his chiselled profile, dazed she should be speaking to him this way but unable to stop.

'*No*, Roslynn,' he said gently, though his fingers had clenched themselves on the shutter.

'No to the warning or no to Roslynn?'

'Both.' He glanced down at her sideways. In her flat walking shoes she barely came to his shoulder, her grey eyes shimmering, lingering in his.

'Have you ever let yourself love a woman?' she asked.

'Maybe I'm not made for the violent passions.'

'You *are*.'

'And how would you know, little one? You have a very virginal air.'

'Don't be angry with me.' With his head thrown back and his eyes wary he looked much more arrogant than usual.

'I'm not.' He went as if to touch her and checked himself. 'May I ask why you're trying to tempt me?'

'That's just it!' she said a little frantically. 'I don't know why I'm the way I am with you at all.'

'No tears,' he ordered.

Roslynn blinked furiously. 'Anyway why are you afraid of me?'

'God knows, Roslynn, I don't want to get into a discussion.'

The curtness of his tone slashed at her like a whip. She even shut her eyes and gave a little stinging cry.

'I've hurt you.' His hands closed around her upper arms. 'I'm sorry.'

'That's all right,' she said faintly. 'I deserve to be put in my place.'

Sholto stooped and kissed her forehead lightly, but something uncontrollable welled up inside her and she turned up her face, her mouth parted.

She felt the tension in his body, the sensual stirring, witnessed the brilliant flash in his eyes. He hauled her right into his arms, driven by her melting, and as she shivered in a darkening ecstasy, brought his mouth down on her own.

It was as if they were both caught up in a swollen current, carried relentlessly along beyond the boundaries of place and time.

'I *won't* hurt you, Roslynn,' she thought she heard him say desperately, but for the first time in her short young life she was Woman drowning Man in her fiery sweetness. His mouth that had lifted so briefly came down on hers again, exploring deeper, sweeping all else aside but pleasure, filling her with so much excitement it became a weakness and she had to cling to him as though she could never let him go.

This being together was like a banquet after starvation, with the same desperation to it. Sholto wrenched his mouth aside, too conscious of her inciting little sounds, cries that were echoed from her bounding heart.

'So now we know I'm human,' he glinted.

'*Sholto*.' Her voice was the softest, yearning plea for understanding.

'Don't you see I can't *do* this?' His handsome face looked wrenched, the blue-green eyes turned to jade.

'No matter. I had a moment.' She looked very beautiful and a little strange. 'Don't send me away, *please*. I promise I'll be sensible for the rest of my life.'

'And what about *me*?' He had to hold her firmly so she wouldn't fall.

'You might decide you like kissing me.'

Despite himself he laughed. 'That's even more serious. You know, Roslynn, with the veil removed you're a witch.'

'Some people might think it fun having a witch around.' She looked intensely into his face, loving it. Loving him. Everything about her ached for this man.

'A witch who won't let a man alone,' he observed shrewdly.

'I'll give you my word.' The shadowy light gleamed on her pearly skin.

'I daren't trust it.' His hands were on her narrow waist, spanning it with his long fingers.

Without even thinking she was going to do it, Roslynn leaned forward and laid her glowing head against his breast. 'I'm really very harmless, Sholto. I wish everything that's good for you.' Her delicate breasts were pressed against him and her eyes were closed.

'What we're considering, little one,' he said dryly.

'is what's good for *you*. Romantic interludes in the summerhouse are most certainly going to be *out*.'

'Whatever you want,' she said. 'I'm not a free agent.'

In the end, because they had arrived at the most unbearable stalemate, Sholto took Vanessa and her son back to the city with him. Vanessa had been white-faced and tight-lipped, barely containing her inner raging.

'I guess I've been rather scared of Aunt Vanessa for too long,' Roslynn later told Elizabeth.

Elizabeth herself thought they would never get rid of the woman, but underneath her fragile exterior Roslynn too was made of steel. They stood watching until the Daimler disappeared and Elizabeth said quickly: 'What about a cup of tea?'

'A good idea.' Roslynn abandoned her staring, remembering Kenneth's face as he had said goodbye to her. Years of happy little incidents came to her mind, all blotted out by a desperate tragedy. Kenneth's unhappy hazel eyes, quiet and unsmiling, the terrible hurt at the back of them. Aunt Vanessa had given her six months to, as she put it, even herself out.

'This isn't *your* country,' she had told Roslynn on the side, 'or *your* family. These people are kind, I'll grant you, because you're small and pathetic and the good doctor saved your life. Just leave when you see the warning signs and cable us your arrival.'

A month went by, a remarkably beautiful and quiet month, while the weather continued almost perfectly. Roslynn continued to explore the old house and the mountainside, feeling more relaxed and happy than she had been in a very long time. Elizabeth was the perfect companion, there when you wanted her, busy with her own pursuits when the spirit craved a little solitude, the honorary grandmother Roslynn craved with all her heart. By the end of the month, Roslynn loved the place as much as Elizabeth did, though both of them missed Sholto badly.

He hadn't come, though he spoke to both women frequently on the telephone. His professional ethic was precious to him, Roslynn considered, and he clearly thought it best to stay away. Still, they never lacked visitors; people driving up to see Elizabeth, the man who delivered the groceries and stayed to have a cup of tea with Annie, not an ordinary man but a successful business man who had suffered a heart attack and given it all up to retreat to the mountain. The stories he told, and the deals, made Roslynn and Annie look forward eagerly to his visits. Then there was Kris, home on vacation from university. He was the grandson of their nearest neighbours and Elizabeth had known him all his life.

'A nice boy,' she told Roslynn, after Roslynn had confided she had met a Kris Neilsen on one of her walks. 'I expect he'll be coming over to see me. *And* you,' she looked up to smile. 'How did his exams go?'

'Oh, great!' Roslynn gave an expressive imitation of Kris's attractive style.

The very next day, Kris turned up and Elizabeth

waved them off as Kris swept Roslynn away in his car.

'She's a great lady!' Kris cried, braking with an abruptness that made Roslynn doubly glad of her seat belt. 'Drat it, did you see that bird? You'd think they were in a crossing.' The birds, in fact, were very tame due no doubt to the active encouragement. 'Sorry, did I give you a fright?'

'It might be as well if we go a little slower.'

'Yes, ma'am.' Kris took his eye off the drive to smile at her admiringly. 'Why didn't Gran tell me there was a girl up here like you? I'd have come up a week sooner.'

'Well,' Roslynn said consideringly, 'it's possible she knew that.'

'Now what does that mean?' Kris raised his fair brows. 'Elizabeth wouldn't have let you come with me, under any circumstances, if she didn't know I was a perfect gentleman.'

'Don't let me rattle you,' she smiled.

'Come to think of it,' he said briskly, 'you're beautiful—and that glorious English skin!'

'I'd much rather have a tan.'

'For gosh sakes,' he groaned, 'don't do it. Haven't you heard of sun cancer?'

'I notice *you're* very brown,' she commented. 'Everyone is.'

'It may be sexy on men, but I like *my* girls with beautiful white skin—and now we mention it, wine-coloured hair.'

'Where are you taking me?' Roslynn asked, mock solemnly.

'Oh, around,' Kris said vaguely. 'There's lots for

you to see and I know a beaut place where we can have lunch.'

It turned out to be the most enjoyable, relaxing day. Kris seemed to be delighted with her, the way she looked and the way she talked, 'that marvellous Pommy accent', like the new novelty in his life. As for Roslynn, though Kris attracted her as an intelligent and lighthearted companion, she had the odd feeling, though she was younger by a year, that she was at least a lifetime removed. So much had happened to her, whereas Kris had led a blissful, blameless life. He talked about his parents, a moving tribute, his career, 'following in the footsteps of Dad', by all accounts a leading architect, the special love he had for his grandparents, his love of the mountain, the great friends in his life, male and female, plenty of each, but when he wanted to talk about Roslynn she was quite unable to respond in the same manner.

'You're a mysterious little creature, aren't you?' he said, taking her hand across the open-air table. 'Well, if you won't talk about yourself, let's talk about Sholto. Now there's a great guy. I mean, he's brilliant. You want to hear people talk about him from the old days when he went to university! Not many like that come along to dazzle us. Did all his postgrad work overseas and was equally impressive there. Just the thought of being a neurosurgeon makes me go weak at the knees. I nearly pass out every time I have to have a needle. I won't even have one at the dentist's.'

'It's different when you have no choice.'

'Of course,' Kris responded sympathetically. 'Here's me talking about needles when you've had an operation. I'll bet you were glad it was Sholto. He's the most committed man I've ever known. Even more than Dad. At least Dad took time off to get married and have me, but the women have been chasing Sholto for years. Have you met that Laura yet?'

'No.' Roslynn wanted to talk about Laura. 'Tell me about her,' she invited.

'A gentleman doesn't talk. Anyway, I don't really feel guilty because I don't like Laura at all. Neither does Elizabeth. No one calls *her* Lady McNaughton unless thay step out of line, but there would be no way we wouldn't all have to call dear Laura Lady McNaughton when the time arrives. Sholto's a bit young for a knighthood yet. What is he? Dad's forty-five, so Sholto is about ten years younger. Anyway, I can see it all happening, can't you?'

'What?'

'Oh, my little darling!' Kris piled more salad on his plate, 'I'm sure if you'd even *seen* Laura you would. Mum says she was nuts about Sholto even when she was married. Exactly!' He caught Roslynn's dismayed expression. 'It appears she, like many others, pursued Sholto in vain, then when it looked as if she was definitely going to be left on the shelf, she married one of his friends.'

'Oh, too bad!'

'You're looking as if you wish I hadn't told you.'

'On the contrary, I'm waiting to hear more.'

'Well,' said Kris, settling happily into his story,

'Laura is one of those pencil-slim blondes. A bit on the gaunt side but always looking perfect. Mum says she's beautiful, but I can't see it. Of course she's not young. She's over thirty, but she's terribly refined. You know the type. Now that Sholto hasn't married anyone else, she appropriated him for her very own. Mum says,' Kris leaned forward and hissed it, 'she's not half good enough for Sholto, but Dad says, who the hell is? and they're friends. The thing is, the men like Laura, but Mum says men understand nothing.'

'Are you trying to tell me they might get married?' Roslynn stared back at him wide-eyed.

'I know!' Kris sighed. 'Call it terrible if you want to. Probably she'd make the ideal partner. Sholto, as you might have noticed, is first and last dedicated to his profession and Mum says the woman in his life would have to be a saint!'

'Why?' Roslynn demanded.

Kris waved his fork vaguely. 'Just Mum's general assessment of the situation. We're all very interested in Sholto, his career and his future. He belongs to all of us, but Laura's different. She would spoil everything. There's more to being attractive than looking good.'

There was indeed, Roslynn thought dismally. Of course Sholto had to have a woman in his life. The right woman. What a fool she was in her schoolgirl daydream! Humiliation burned in her.

'Look here, you're looking positively unnerved,' Kris said anxiously.

'I simply can't take it all in.'

Kris moved back so his fair head was framed against the blue sky. 'Say, you haven't got a crush on Sholto, have you?' he looked deeply into her crystalline eyes.

'At the moment he's my doctor.'

'Women are always falling in love with their doctors,' Kris pointed out briskly. 'Mum said she couldn't even count on not falling in love with Sholto. I mean, did you ever see such a terrific-looking guy, and he's almost absurdly unaware of it.'

'I expect he's got far more important things for ever on his mind,' said Roslynn.

Other people were coming into the courtyard of the restaurant, and under the waves and smiles and fleeting introductions Roslynn had time to get fully in control of herself. The last thing she wanted was to make her feelings for Sholto conspicuous, though strangely she didn't mind Elizabeth knowing. Elizabeth was the same as a dear grandmother, she sighed with relief.

'Hi there, old pal!' Another attractive young man stopped by their table, looking pointedly at Roslynn. 'I say now, who's this?'

'*My* girl,' Kris returned none too jovially.

'Are you going to introduce us?' the other boy laughed, not embarrassed.

'No.'

'You've never been the possessive type before.'

'Don't you see we can ask nothing better than to be alone?' snapped Kris.

'Oh, all right,' the young man started to move off and as he did so bent down to whisper to Roslynn,

'Don't worry, I'll find some excuse to stop on the way back.'

'Who's that?' she asked afterwards, smiling.

'The mountain's Casanova,' Kris told her gloomily. 'You'll be seeing him again, of course. His family always come up here for Christmas.'

'What I meant was, what's his real name?'

'Luke Edwards.' Kris's blue eyes drifted to Luke's table. 'If you want to know, he's Laura Edward's nephew by marriage.'

'Now there's a crazy coincidence,' Roslynn said.

Over the next week, Roslynn saw a lot of Kris and he took her over to their own high villa to meet his mother, who looked incredibly young to have such a big, handsome son.

'A child bride,' she explained. Jenny Neilsen was a very lively, gossipy sort of woman, tall and blonde, like her son, and like Kris very warm and agreeable. She took an immediate liking to Roslynn, a feeling that was mutual, and in the presence of that lady Roslynn found out more about the inhabitants of the mountain than she ever could world affairs from a taxi driver. She knew everybody who came there for the summer; writers, painters, politicians, a retired opera singer, big business men who had to take a break or go into intensive care . . . oh, *everyone*! There were always a lot of parties over the Christmas and New Year break, and already Jenny had begun telephoning.

'God only knows when Laura will arrive,' she told Roslynn in a suspenseful voice. 'Of course we'll have to invite her to our party. Duty before pleasure.'

'If she's as cold as you say, why does Sholto like her?' Roslynn asked, mystified.

'*Pet!*' Jenny's clear mezzo went faint. 'I didn't say she was cold to *Sholto*. She prefers Sholto to anyone else in the world. Oh, look, your coffee's all gone. I'll get you some more.'

Kris drove her home, late afternoon, making jokes, digging out all his little anecdotes one by one, wondering how Roslynn looked so chaste and so sexy at one and the same time. He would have liked her to linger so he could examine every feature of that enchanting triangular face, but she turned to him with a smile.

'Thank you for a beautiful day. I really like your mother. She's very kind and funny.'

'She likes you too, kid.' Obeying an entirely uncontrollable impulse, Kris leaned over and kissed her briefly but enthusiastically. 'There, did that make you happy?'

She looked back at him through her veiled lashes. 'I thought you said Luke was the mountain's Casanova?'

'I couldn't help it,' he said with a broad smile. 'You know how it is?'

'More or less.' She didn't wait for him to come around to her side of the car, but sprang out as gracefully as a gazelle. 'Drive carefully.'

'I assure you, my lady, I will.' Kris gave her a wave, then shot away like a rally driver.

Roslynn sat down beside the stone fountain and tried to wriggle the little pebbles that had bounced up out of her sandal. Kris was a really terrible driver. She had to control herself not to tell him.

Someone came down the front stairs as she was bending over the clasp and she looked up expecting to see Elizabeth.

'Oh, it's you!' she exclaimed, feeling so lightheaded she swayed.

Sholto moved quickly, sitting down beside her and putting a steadying arm around her. 'You surprised me.' There was no other way she could disguise her own weakness.

'Here, show me.' He slipped her sandal off and shook it out. 'Kris can't seem to get the hang of a smooth take-off, but I guess he's smooth enough in other directions.'

'You saw him kiss me?' She peered anxiously at his dark profile.

'I'm sorry, wasn't I supposed to?' With no effort at all he had the tiny catch on her sandal buckled up again.

'It was just kid stuff,' she protested.

Now it was his turn to stare at her and she felt the colour rush up under her skin. He had changed his city clothes and the beautiful blue of his casual shirt had invaded his brilliant eyes. 'And you're an authority?'

'I'm as safe as I could be with Kris.'

'Tell me.'

'He's a very nice boy.'

'But of course he is,' Sholto agreed. 'It's his driving that's all wrong.'

'He's not reckless,' Roslynn defended Kris earnestly. 'It's just that he has no feeling for machinery.'

'At least you've managed to see something of the countryside,' Sholto remarked kindly.

'Are you angry with me or something?' she asked him.

'No, I'm not.' He took her chin in his hand. 'Let me have a look at you.'

'Why didn't you tell us you were coming?' she challenged him. 'It would have been something to look forward to.'

He looked down at her steadily and whatever else she was trying to say slipped away. From the very first moment she had set eyes on him he had elicited this tremendous response. Everything about him entranced her, the wholeness, the brilliance and sensitivity, intentness and dedication, his unconsciousness of himself, that stunning male aura that made people look and look again. Perhaps he was a bit too stunning, she thought fervently. This close he took her breath away.

'And what have you decided?' he asked her.

She shook her head. 'I'm sure you've heard it lots of times.'

'Heard what?' he smiled at her.

'That's a nice shirt.' She looked at his brown throat. There was an elegance about him no matter what he wore, his height, his body, as lean as an athlete's.

'It's old, if you want to know.'

He would take her for an utter fool. She jumped up from the low brick wall and turned to face away from him. It was the only way she could keep her head. 'I was terrified my . . . awkwardness might have kept you away.'

'I can't remember any awkwardness, Roslynn,' Sholto said lightly.

'In any case, I'm over it.' She spoke the words quickly, compulsively, to reassure him.

'And what are you over anyway?' He stood up, smiling slightly, resting his two hands on her shoulders.

'The embarrassing subject that kept you away.'

His eyes rested on her downbent, glowing head, the flushed cheeks and the straight line of her short nose. 'I stayed away,' he told her sardonically, 'so you could achieve harmony within yourself.'

'Make me come to my senses, you mean.'

'No,' he answered her without mockery. 'So you wouldn't spend your emotions at a time when you were obviously so frail. That would only have taken a heavy toll of your strength.'

'I'm feeling much better now,' she interrupted, a little desperately.

'I can see that.' He gave her one of his lancing glances. 'Thriving on attention.'

'I'm not interested in Kris,' she said quickly, rather bothered by some glint in his eyes.

'Just as well,' he said pleasantly. 'He wouldn't suit you at all.'

'I'd be intensely grateful to you if you would point out somebody who *would*,' she said recklessly, reacting to his arrogance.

'Surely you don't want to suffer the madness of a love affair?'

'I want *everything*,' she said. 'Madness, marriage, children I can love.'

'You're too young to get married,' Sholto answered her, purposely cool.

'How do *you* know?'

'I'm certain of it,' he said dryly. 'Do you know your eyes are flashing?'

'Are they?' Rosslyn bent her head. 'You make me feel very frustrated at times.'

'You're still being too sensitive,' he said, noting how the sunlight was making small flames of her hair. It had lengthened considerably, curling around her small head in a rosy nimbus. 'Shall we go for a walk, or are you too tired?'

'But I'm not tired at all.' The heady sweet scents of the garden were all round them and she looked up into his jewel-coloured eyes. 'It seems like a miracle that you've come.'

'Roslynn.' There was a strange tautness in his voice.

'It's all right!' She spread out her small hands. 'I always stick to my promises. I said I'll act sensibly and I will. You can't imagine how we've missed you.'

Sholto offered her his hand and she took it at once, both of them taking the path that led to the wisteria walk. Being in love was the most extraordinary state, Roslynn thought— a state of total obsession.

It should have been a perfect weekend and it would have been, only Laura Edwards, with quite a classic piece of planning, started her holiday early. She had heard quite enough of Sholto's young guest, had it confirmed over and over that she was exceedingly pretty, and decided to act. In the normal course of events she would have waited for the usual invitation, but so loudly had Luke sung the girl's praises that Laura became positively anxious, a not unnatural reaction. Her whole history had been her unrequited love for Sholto. She had never cared beyond liking for her husband, and with Sholto remaining so long the eligible bachelor Laura had decided it needed real initiative to win him. No young thing, however charming, could be allowed to dazzle Sholto's eyes, when dazzlement was the last thing he wanted. Sholto was an extraordinary man, but he was first and last a doctor. Laura considered herself just right for him.

On the Saturday morning, Laura rang the house, spoke to Elizabeth, who suddenly became dejected but managed to furnish the expected invitation to dinner that evening.

'May I bring Luke along as well?' Laura asked winningly. 'He so much wants to meet your young guest, but I believe Kris Neilsen has been hiding her.'

'We have guests this evening,' said Elizabeth when' she want back into the sunroom.

'Really?' Sholto gave the merest frown. He was reading the paper, delighted by the absence of telephone calls, and Roslynn was tucked up on the cushioned bench around the big bay window, gently stroking the cat.

It was a peaceful, sunlit scene and Elizabeth loathed to break it. In fact it was all she could do not to say, *drat*! But that could never be; instead she said mildly, 'Laura has arrived. I invited her over for dinner. Her nephew too. It appears what little he's seen of Roslynn has filled him with a desire to see more.'

'I'm sure.' Sholto turned his head and gave Roslynn a speaking glance. 'Try as you do, Roslynn, you can't seem to keep a man out of your life.'

'I've only seen him once,' Roslynn murmured, trying to keep a feeling of dismay out of her voice. 'Kris wouldn't even introduce us.'

'I expect he feared the competition.'

'As a matter of fact,' Roslynn confided with flushed cheeks, 'I'm not interested in either of them.'

'Let's get off the subject,' said Elizabeth lightly. 'Darling, would you get me another cup of tea?'

Both Sholto and Roslynn went to get up and Sholto asked amusedly: 'Which one of us are you talking to?'

'Actually, dearest, I was speaking to Roslynn. I wouldn't have the heart to bother you.'

With Sholto standing so close to her, towering over her really, Roslynn felt quite breathless. 'Please, Sholto, I'll fix it.'

'You know,' he said, with a sort of deliberation, 'you're really the little granddaughter Gran always wanted. My sisters are so immensely self-sufficient.'

'And I'm not?' She really had to wear high heels when she was speaking to him.

'What Sholto means, Roslynn,' Elizabeth explained smilingly, 'is that you're endearing. You *give* so much. I love my granddaughters dearly, but what Sholto says has made me realise that they always were very self-contained. I suppose that's why I always loved Sholto best. He's a giver too.'

'Am I going to like Laura?' Roslynn asked when they were all comfortably seated again.

Elizabeth almost choked and Sholto answered for her. 'It would make me happy if you would.'

'Oh.' She couldn't help meeting Elizabeth's eyes and seeing the answering understanding in their dark depths.

'Was that a little sigh?' Sholto asked.

'Not exactly.' Roslynn took to stroking the cat again. 'It was more a wave of emotion. Are you going to marry Laura, Sholto?'

Elizabeth's eyelids drooped a little, but she very clearly wanted to know as well.

'What a question!' he said carelessly, folding the paper and putting it down.

'We're agonising on the answer,' she told him.

'Who, you and Gran?' His head was tilted back and he looked indescribably amused and arrogant at the same time.

'It isn't a crime to tell us, is it?' Roslynn protested.

'I haven't yet made up my mind.' There was a mocking quality to his voice.

'Let me guess.'

'Oh no, I won't.' He moved so quickly both Roslynn and the cat were startled. The cat jumped to the floor and Sholto put his hands on Roslynn's tiny waist, lifting her right out of the window seat. 'I'm going down to the village—coming?'

'If you are, dear, Elizabeth said quickly, 'we'll need a few things from the shops.'

'Sit there,' Sholto said easily, 'I'll ask Annie.'

In the end, Annie had quite a list. Cooking for the

family was one thing, but as Annie had good reason to recall, Laura was a very fussy eater and rather into that new French cuisine where there wasn't a sauce on anything. They had been going to have stuffed leg of lamb wrapped in puff pastry with roast potatoes and onions and some nice vegetables for colour, but Annie remembered now that Laura didn't care for lamb or poultry. It would have to be fish. She would bake them whole with macadamia stuffing and maybe a salmon pâté as a starter.

'Look, we're not going to put you to all this bother,' said Sholto, rather taken aback by the list.

'No bother, Mr McNaughton,' Annie assured him. 'I daresay you would have preferred the lamb?'

'*I* would,' Roslynn said irrepressibly, 'but anything you cook, Annie, tastes good.'

'May *I* drive the car?' Roslynn asked when they had made their way to the garage.

'What?' Sholto looked down on her, feigning amazement.

'Don't you trust me?'

'No.'

'Actually I'm a good driver,' she said, quite hurt.

'I just don't mean driving.'

'*Oh.*' There was something different about him. She could see it from the disturbing gleam in his eyes.

'Are you going to get in?' he asked suavely, and held open the driver's door.

'I've driven a Daimler before. There's nothing to worry about.'

'Well, I *am* worried, if you want to know.'

'All right, then, I won't.' Roslynn looked back at him over her shoulder.

'Don't be stupid, get in.'

They were down the long driveway and out on to the road before Sholto spoke again.

'You're right, you *are* a good driver, though it's difficult to drive this car badly.'

'Thank you,' she retorted sweetly.

'Tell me when those little wrists get tired.'

'Listen, I'm five feet two!'

'And very pretty. Don't get upset, little one. I'm only teasing.'

'I'm not used to it from *you*,' she explained. 'You're usually rather severe—the distinguished neuro-surgeon.'

'It's less dangerous.'

'Now what does that mean?' she asked.

'Don't take your eyes off the road!'

'You glance at me,' she pointed out mildly.

'Perhaps. I prefer it that way.'

Nothing could spoil her happy mood. Not even the advent of Laura. She could feel herself smiling, her grey eyes large and luminous.

'You're healing aren't you?' Sholto commented.

'I feel well.'

'I mean in yourself, the sustaining spirit.'

'I have you and Elizabeth to thank for that. And Annie and Bill. Annie feeds me up and Bill lets me help him with all the little alpine flowers.'

'You're rather like a flower yourself, but Annie hasn't fattened you up.'

'Are you *mad?*' Roslynn exclaimed. 'I've put on four pounds!'

'Where?' His brilliant gaze slipped all over her.

'The details must remain quiet.'

By the time they reached the village they had settled into a kind of banter that was to be sustained for weeks. Sholto was teasing, indulgent, rather like a favourite, superior big brother, until she turned around on him rather swiftly and caught that disturbing glint in his eyes. Then every pulse in her body went crazy and she wanted him to crush her up against him and kiss her as he had done once before. She even supposed her eyes were transparent, for his own eyes were alight with unmistakable understanding. He *knew* she loved him. She could almost see his mind working. How could he make everything come out beautifully and still not hurt her? At least something about her was precious to him—her wellbeing.

They didn't divide up the shopping but did it together, Sholto greeted with warmth and a telling edge of respect on all sides. There was something about him that deterred people from becoming overly friendly, but he was evidently highly regarded, even worshipped, like the local deity.

It made Roslynn laugh because she saw it so very clearly.

'Now what's amusing you?' Sholto turned his head quickly and looked straight down into her eyes.

'I'm simply observing how people react to you.'

'They don't give me a lot of cheek like you.'

'And it seems to me you need a little lack of reverence.'

'Ah, yes.' He reached down and took some parcels from her.

'You don't seem quite human enough to me,' Roslynn told him.

'I shouldn't mind that,' he said, 'but I do.'

For an instant she thought she had offended him, then she saw his eyes. 'I'm going to pay for that, aren't I?' she said shakily.

'You shouldn't go around saying the things you do.' He moved off lithely and she had to skip along to match him. 'Why haven't you got a hat on your head?' he suddenly asked abruptly.

'*You* haven't.' She had to stop herself by clutching his arm.

'My dear child, I haven't got camellia skin and red hair.'

'Well, let's get one, then,' she challenged him. 'I've been wearing Elizabeth's gardening hat and it's not very glamorous.'

He only looked at her dryly. 'Oh, I think it would be on you.'

They piled all the parcels into the car, then they retraced their steps to a little shop that sold everything one could think of that could be made out of straw.

'What about this?'

'Perfect.' She took the sun-yellow, wide-brimmed straw hat off him, plonking it down on her head.

'You *could* take the time to settle it,' he said, twirling the brim so the yellow scarf that encircled it now had its ends to the back.

'I'll have to use you for a mirror. All right?' She

looked up at him for approval, her large eyes heavily lashed and very feminine beneath the wide yellow brim.

'Excellent,' he said briefly, then turned away to pay for it.

He didn't allow her to drive home because he said she had done quite enough, and she sighed gently and threw her new hat on to the back seat. Now their talk wasn't quite so natural and Sholto's handsome dark face was back to being guarded. Or it could have been a trick of the light.

'Thank you for my hat,' Roslynn said when they arrived home, but he only smiled and made no answer. Probably he thought a moment's gratification was a weakness, because as she gazed at herself up in her bedroom she could see the yellow hat flaunted her colouring. Ah well! She was so tremulous inside, so helpless and vulnerable she felt like a bird.

A good part of the afternoon was given over to preparations for their little dinner party, and Elizabeth insisted that Roslynn arrange all the flowers because 'you make such a good job of them'.

Searching out various blossoms for a mixed arrangement, she suddenly gave a whimper of pain.

'What *is* it?' Sholto, who had just come through the doorway, rounded on her with an urgency quite out of proportion to her injury.

'Oh, help!' She stretched out her hand. 'A bee's stung me.'

'God, you frightened me,' he said simply. He took her hand in a gentle, firm grasp and looked at the faint swelling. 'An antihistamine will fix that.'

'Have we got one?' Roslynn wore an expression of childlike alarm.

'Follow me.' He led her through the house to the downstairs bathroom where a large medicine chest adorned the far wall.

'I believe it's getting bigger,' she said.

'Yes.' He smeared a little soothing cream over the area, his head bent over her own.

'I hate bee stings,' she said, quite understanding she had to say something when she was so conscious of his touch.

'You're not allergic.'

'I expect you know everything,' she sighed.

'Not about *you*, Roslynn.'

And there it was again, the strange disturbance. She lifted her head quickly and met his eyes, but after the briefest moment he turned away and sought an antihistamine tablet, making her swallow it with a half tumbler of water.

'Thank you,' she said, quickly flushing. At certain moments he made her feel more helpless and vulnerable than ever. The schoolgirl agonisingly in love with an unattainable hero figure.

'You've gone rather white,' Sholto told her.

'Have I?' Even her voice trembled.

'Gran can finish the flowers.'

'Don't be silly, I'm fit enough to paint the house.'

'It needs a paint really.'

They were both talking aimlessly to mask some shared current of feeling, a sick desire on hers, probably a wry pity on his. With every faculty so acute he could sense what she was feeling as well as seeing her trembling.

She withdrew her hand quickly, not without a certain struggle. 'I must get back to the flowers, you know,' she said crisply, to convince him. 'I expect Laura always sets a gracious table.'

'After looking at what you've done, she doesn't arrange flowers half so well.'

'Well, that's something,' she said meaningfully. 'I'm looking forward to meeting Laura a great deal.'

CHAPTER SEVEN

As it turned out, Roslynn couldn't take to Laura Edwards at all. Worse, Laura even reminded her strongly of Vanessa. There was more than a superficial resemblance. They were of the same physical type; tall, pencil-slim, golden-haired and light-eyed. Roslynn had to check herself from running back to her room.

'Ah, yes, your little guest,' said Laura, taking Roslynn's hand. 'Just please don't break my nephew's heart.'

So that little opening gambit placed Roslynn just where Laura wanted her to be, the teenage guest grouped off with the young nephew. The nephew was now saying something, his eyes very bright. Clearly Laura had decided it was necessary to interest Roslynn in her own age group.

'I've been dying to meet you all week,' Luke Edwards confided. 'Not easy with Kris around.' Good-looking as he was, there was something faintly unpleasing about his face, Roslynn decided. His features were good, but there was a shallowness somewhere as if his athletic appearance was pretty well all he had to offer. Kris appealed to her very much more.

After a pre-dinner drink they went in to dinner, Luke taking her arm with a too-easy gesture. She couldn't possibly embarrasss him by jerking it away, but she wanted to. She moved her eyes ahead to where Laura and Sholto were standing by the beautiful double cedar doors. Though a tall woman, Laura still had to tilt her head up to speak to him and her blue eyes were alight with the very special feeling she had for him.

Another one, Roslynn thought, and for a moment even felt heartbroken for Laura and for herself. Sholto was married to a demanding profession. A woman would *have* to come second in his life. Stupid women, falling in love with these devastating men. Laura's clear-skinned, fine-featured, rather glacial type face was now liquid with deep feeling, her eyes locked in Sholto's as though powerless to look away.

Luke shrugged. 'I expect they'll make a match of it shortly,' he observed in an undertone. 'I should say fairly early in the New Year. I know Laura is hoping.'

Roslynn nodded. One couldn't live without hope. She was grateful now that she wasn't wearing anything Laura had selected. Not that Laura had indulged in evening wear on her behalf. She was wearing her own dress, the only thing suitable in the limited wardrobe she had brought from England. Sholto had had her things taken out of storage and sent up to her. Mercifully, as it turned out, she possessed something that could hold its own against Laura's classic elegance. And Laura, like Vanessa, was exquisitely turned out, blonde hair pulled back rather austerely, but it suited her, pale skin exceedingly matt, not a trace of a natural shine, wearing a black and white silk dress with considerable panache. A top model couldn't have worn it better, and her long legs were lovely.

For all the trouble Annie had gone to, Laura barely pecked at her food. She was far from being vivacious, her style being languid, but she was confident, intelligent, immersed in her host, charming to his grandmother, and prepared to show an interest in their little English house guest.

'I expect you'll be going home after you explore some more of Australia?' she questioned Roslynn pleasantly.

'There's no hurry at all,' Elizabeth interjected, because she knew the whole business worried Roslynn more than it ought to. 'We want Roslynn to pick up very much more before she does a lot of travelling.'

'But she looks so *well*,' Laura exclaimed, inwardly dismayed to find the English girl so lovely. She had counted on someone a whole lot near the young girls she knew, someone very pretty (she had after all been warned) but still growing out of the gawky stage. There was nothing at all green or gawky about this girl. She spoke beautifully and she was very poised.

After dinner they retreated to the drawing room for coffee and liqueurs and Luke seated himself beside Roslynn on the silk upholstered love-seat asking her if she would care to come over to his place the following afternoon.

'Perhaps another time,' she said defensively. 'Sholto said we might be going out.'

'Where to?' asked Luke, his smile sharpening.

'I don't really know. He merely said out.'

But Luke wasn't prepared to leave it there. He turned his dark brown head to quiz Sholto.

'Where are you taking Roslynn tomorrow afternoon?' he asked with his habitual brand of boldness.

'Sholto!' Laura protested. Had she, too, something lined up?

Roslynn swallowed quickly, trying to keep the anxiety out of her face. What if Sholto betrayed surprise or said they weren't going anywhere?

Sholto didn't even hesitate. 'Actually I'm taking her back to town with me,' he said smoothly. 'I want her to have a thorough check-up?'

'With *you*, Sholto?' Laura asked in a voice that almost failed her.

'Not entirely. I've made an appointment for her to see Nick Grosvenor. He's the best physician there is. It's good to see Roslynn looking so well and recovered, but post-operative check-ups are important.'

'Yes, of course.' Elizabeth seconded emphatically not uttering one word of her own surprise. 'A little bit of city life will do her good, and she can do some Christmas shopping.'

'So where will you stay?' Laura asked in a pleasant tone.

'At the house, of course,' Elizabeth jumped in, yet again. 'Mrs Harper will be there to look after her.'

'I'm sure you know how lucky you are, Roslynn,' Laura smiled. 'Sholto and Lady McNaughton must be the kindest people in the world.'

Behind the smile Roslynn knew there was confusion and torment, yet Laura maintained her mask of urbanity for the rest of the evening. Luke wasn't enjoying himself either. He had thought he had only to meet Roslynn properly to secure her interest. He had always had plenty of girls and found it easy enough, so Roslynn's apparent lack of interest was unexpected to say the least. Perhaps it made her feel better to play hard to get. At least it made a change! Big silver eyes as cool as the rain, Luke was convinced, like all girls, she was only playing a game.

'See you when you get back,' he told her as they were leaving, his bright eyes dropping persistently to her mouth. He would love to kiss her; destroy that cool.

'You didn't tell us when?' Laura murmured, turning fully to face Sholto.

'Next weekend, if I can arrange it.'

'Do you ever take a holiday?' Laura asked. She had reached the stage when she was finding it very hard to accept that Sholto's interest in his precious little patient was entirely professional.

'I'm thinking about it this year.' Sholto looked indolently down on her and she stretched out her hand and just brushed his cheek.

'You deserve one, Sholto. You can't put your own health in jeopardy.'

Roslynn looked at them both and looked away. As Sholto was looking the very picture of male beauty and vigour Laura's concern sounded comical. When it was time for Laura to say goodnight to Roslynn there was a definite shadow in the pale, blue eyes.

'Enjoy your shopping, my dear,' Laura said graciously. 'I don't think I thanked you for your little thank-you note.'

'It was very kind of you to help me out,' Roslynn responded.

'I'd do anything for *Sholto*,' Laura stressed very lightly. 'We've been friends for a long time.'

'So that's the beauteous Laura,' Roslynn remarked quietly to Elizabeth as Sholto walked their guests down to their car.

'What did you think?' Elizabeth shifted so she could see the girl's face.

'Very . . . elegant.' Roslynn hesitated very faintly. 'It's the oddest thing, but she reminds me of Aunt Vanessa—not in manner but in appearance.'

'I thought you'd see it straight away. Sholto said you were bound to.'

'Then you noticed it as well.'

'*I'll* say!' said Elizabeth.

A couple of hours later, Roslynn was finding it impossible to sleep. The evening's conversation was whirling around in her head. All right, so Laura looked like Aunt Vanessa, so what? So all her unhappy memories came back to haunt her. Her head began to ache with a dull pain and she nursed it to herself for a while, then decided to get a couple of her tablets. She hadn't taken them for weeks. After a few moments searching her top drawer she remembered where she had left them. In the medicine chest downstairs, of course. It nearly put her off getting them, only she didn't fancy her chances of sleeping without them.

Moonlight poured through the tall stained glass window above the landing. She could see the outline of furniture clearly, the marble-topped console, the mirror that hung above it, the antique Chinese vases and the two rosewood chairs. Over the course of the weeks she had become very familiar with the house, loving it almost as if it belonged to her. Yet she too had a beautiful house, furnished on an even grander scale. The only thing she could think of doing with it was leaving Aunt Vanessa there as a tenant. It was much too early to go home yet.

The house was virtually in darkness, yet she found her way easily. The light filled the bathroom with so much brightness she had to blink. It took her less than a minute to find the tablets and she shook two out on her hand. Her head was aching harder now and she gave a soft little moan. Just let these work, she prayed. For over a month now she had been thrusting her problems below her calm surface; now, tonight, they were back to plague her.

Footsteps echoed along the passageway and as she turned, glass in hand, there was Sholto at the door.

'What is it, Roslynn, a headache?' Those too intelligent eyes took in everything, her physical and mental state.

'A bit of a one,' she shrugged almost guiltily.

'How many tablets are you taking?' He came to her and opened out her palm. 'All right, swallow them down.'

She turned away from him and did so, and when she put the glass down she caught her reflection in the mirror. A small girl in a blue nightgown and robe, pale face dominated by eyes that looked silver, the pupils distended to betray her emotional excitement. No matter how stiltedly she had answered him she was continually seeking ways to fight down the emotional excesses he aroused in her.

'Sit down for a few moments,' he pulled the chair towards her and leant back against the red cedar bench vanity. 'Couldn't you sleep?'

'No.' Roslynn lifted her hands and clasped her temples.

'You haven't had headaches for weeks?'

'No, I told you.' She was speaking rather shortly, because she was trying hard to keep control over herself. The light above them gleamed in her hair, curling back from her white temples and up from a very vulnerable-looking nape. He was gazing at her with true perception, his voice quiet and concerned, but the mere aura of his male presence was enough to set up a clamour in her blood.

Damn Sholto! she thought in a moment of torment. Keeping himself inviolate, can't be bothered with women except as patients. It was grossly unfair, but she couldn't contain her hurt.

After a few moments he came behind her and began to very gently massage sections of her scalp.

'*Oh!*' Whatever he was doing, the headache seemed to be vanishing.

'You must relax your nervous system, Roslynn,' he told her. 'Make yourself perfectly calm in mind and body. It can be done, though it usually takes a long time for Westerners.'

She tilted back her head with her eyes closed, not for a moment intending provocation, seeking only the benefit of the power source that flowed from his hands. 'That's *perfect*! Go on.'

Inexplicably his hands stopped and as her eyes flew open their gaze met. 'You have to go to bed. It's nearly one o'clock.'

Surely she imagined the faint sensual hostility in his face? Though the bones of Sholto's face were very ascetic, his mouth wasn't. It was a good mouth, firm with very clean-cut edges, but it had the outline of a man of passion.

Funny for Sholto, she thought with a terrible wave of shame. Was this the way he thought she was trying to repay him for saving her life, for showering on her all these kindnesses? Inexcusable provocation?

Her eyes filled with tears and she knocked his hands away frantically. She was out of the chair with a despairing little cry, catching the hem of her robe but not caring. Why couldn't she make herself see things as they really were? Sholto was thirty-five, by far the more worldly, experienced, wise and mature. She was nineteen, neither a woman nor a child and she was plaguing him with her obsessive love. A love he neither wanted nor wished to handle.

'Roslynn!' He caught her before she ever reached

the door and she spun around in his arms and hit him.

'Let me go!' To her intense distress she couldn't find control.

'This is senseless—you know that, don't you?'

'So why don't you let me run?' She could hardly see him for the tears in her eyes.

'*Stop it!*' He caught her flailing, fragile hands.

'I hate you, Sholto,' she said passionately, because now in a way she did hate him.

'You don't.' His voice was harsh and clipped, barely recognisable as his usual calm tone.

'If you don't let me go,' she said wildly, 'I'll scream!'

'Then there's only one way to stop that.' He took her head between his hands not gently, but forcibly at last, bringing his mouth down punishingly on the tender softness of hers. He even seemed to be another person or he yielded to his own nature, kissing her in a way she was never likely to forget.

Her blood surged like fire and, beyond reason, she pressed herself to him, his hands dropping as he pulled her to him, binding her against his sleek, male body. For one moment she thought she would faint, so explosive were her feelings. She knew that he wanted her; wanted to punish her, but truly she didn't care. This was ecstasy, however fleetingly she had it.

His hands were on her body now, possessive and passionate. They shaped her breasts, the delicate curves, the aroused peaks and her response was so acute her legs buckled under her. She would have fallen, only he lifted her helpless in his arms. His fabulous face looked strange, almost ablaze.

She was completely at his mercy, realising for the first time that he was one thousand times more demanding than she had ever imagined. She in her schoolgirl fantasy. Why, she couldn't match him, her heart beating frantically.

'Is that what you wanted?' He looked down at her, something alien in the familiar brilliance of his eyes.

Roslynn tried to say something but couldn't, her arms linked tightly around his neck. She had longed for him as a lover; now she was frightened, elated, her wide eyes regarding him as a conqueror.

'You're just a baby,' Sholto said, still in that harsh, jarring tone. 'A baby with a head full of dreams.'

He carried her up the stairs in darkness, her body feverish, weightless, stunned yet melting. She couldn't believe this with any other human being, but whatever Sholto wanted she didn't care. Complex though he was, she was Sholto's for all her life. Never mind if he sent her to the other side of the earth! If she never saw him again, he would matter until the day she died.

The light was still on in her bedroom and he almost tossed her on the bed, fortunately so soft she sank like a feather.

'No, I'm not going to take you,' he said curtly, answering the breathless question in her eyes. 'I may want you very badly, but I'm not likely to forget everything. You're here in my home, under my protection. You may force me to kiss you, now you're helpless.'

He was quite right, she was. Her eyes were glowing like jewels, yet there was fear in them, fear of the first time, fear that couldn't match that electrifying power.

Very abruptly he pulled the sheet over her and she clutched at his wrist compulsively. 'I've made you very angry.'

'Yes, I think you have.'

'Then you'll want to send me away.'

'The sooner the better.'

'I won't go.' Half senseless with excitement, she came off the bed at him, subsiding abruptly against his hard torso. In moments she had become his creation, not a girl he had taken in, but part of him.

'Roslynn.' His hands held her off so fiercely the thin strap of her nightgown was ripped.

'I can't bear to go,' she said brokenly. 'I know I'm pitiful, but I seem to be beyond caring.'

'Oh, dear God!' Now, amazingly, he was cradling her while she wept against him like an abandoned child.

'I love you, Sholto,' she told him. 'I feel bound to you. I know you hate it.'

'It's *not* love,' he tilted up her face a little. 'You're infatuated, a crush.'

'Oh, *no!*' Why was he speaking to her so tenderly? 'I love you no matter what happens—if you marry Laura or not. If I never see you again. I haven't been free since that very first day. I fell in love with you then. I can't explain why it happened, I know it can never be, but damn it, Sholto, you're my friend.

I've got to be able to talk to you. You've made me dependent on you, and I'm not such a fool I don't know you want me in some way.'

'Oh, I want you,' he said with chilling dispassion.

'But you don't need me. I might get in the way of your work.'

He looked faintly shocked. 'You weren't the only one, Roslynn, who had a presentiment of involvement. Hundreds of women have gained my sympathy, attractive women, but there was never the slightest possibility I could become personally involved. You were different from the start. No one could stop that—not even me, and I've tried.'

She lifted her mouth and pressed it to his throat. 'All right, I'll go. I'll do anything to help you.'

'You can't go,' he said flatly. 'You're not strong enough to go anywhere. There's really only one way I can protect you, and that's marry you.'

'But you know you don't *want* to.' The shock was so incredible it stopped her tears.

'I've already admitted you to my life,' Sholto said sombrely, smoothing his hand rhythmically over the curve of her shoulder.

'And in no time at all I'd be an object of your loathing. No, thank you,' she said violently. 'I'd rather be your mistress than an unloved liability.'

'And how could I have a nineteen-year-old mistress, may I ask?' A trace of humour had crept into his brilliant eyes.

'That's it, forever considering your reputation!'

'People are beginning to talk about you already,' he said gravely. 'You're a very beautiful girl,

Roslynn. In itself that's a talking point. Jealousy goads people into saying lots of things. I saw how that boy Luke Edwards looked at you—the way he looked at both of us. Laura, too, was lost in her thoughts.'

'And what about Laura?' She stared at him, insisting that he answer.

'My feeling for Laura is the affection of a long acquaintanceship.'

'You know damn well she's in love with you!'

'Being in love suits a lot of women,' he drawled.

The truth of that stung her acutely. 'All right, so your life has been plagued with importunate women trying to make you *see* them.'

'*You* didn't have to try.'

'You could sound more glad if it.'

He smiled but didn't answer, a faint bitterness around his mouth.

'Do you think caring for me is a folly?' she asked, when he was about to turn away.

'I think it's reckless, ill-advised. You're very young. You haven't really had a chance at life. I know the older you get the more spirit and character you're going to develop. You're a very determined little person, a fighter. It pulled you through as much as my skill. You're going to want a man who can give you his whole life, not a man you have to share with a very demanding way of life. Then, when I should be looking after my patients, I might want to be with you. You can see you have power enough now.'

'But you just suggested marriage,' she cried, almost defeated by his remote expression.

'As a means of protection, not living together.'

'That's crazy!'

'No crazier than your saying you wouldn't go. You see, little one, each of us is trapped. Measuring the folly against the inability to let go. I know I would worry about you endlessly if you weren't right under my nose.'

'Then you love me.'

'What does love mean?' he asked soberly, 'beyond the urgencies of the body.'

'It means making a life together. The remainder of our lives. You ought to see that. I know I'm young, Sholto, but there's nothing really unusual about falling in love at once and for ever. You're everything I'll ever want in a man, the confident authority, the caring, if we must forget about how you make me go to pieces. Sexual love isn't an outrage. Do you resent my attraction?'

Glinting lights fanned up in his eyes. 'I'm not recommending desire for a steady hand.'

'In other words, you don't want any drain on your single-mindedness to your career?'

'What are we talking about anyway?' Sholto sighed wearily. 'Get into bed. Your eyes are swallowing up your face.'

'Heaven knows, you're the doctor.'

'It does make things . . . difficult.' He adjusted the pillows so she was lying more comfortably.

'Well,' she clasped his hand, 'aren't you going to kiss me goodnight?'

'Forget it,' he said gently.

'I suppose I can pretend if you can.' It was good

to see a smile replace the grim remoteness. 'Are you still taking me tomorrow, or is that plan all over as well?'

His voice became coolly professional and he switched off the bedside lamp. 'I did make an appointment with Grosvenor for you and I want to run a few checks myself. You remember? You're my responsibility.'

'Even so, there's one thing you're forgetting, Sholto,' she told him simply, 'someone has to care for you too. If there's only going to be a fraction of a second that you want someone to lean on, I'd like to be there.'

'Would you?' His beautiful mouth twisted wryly.

'I know what I'm saying,' she said strongly. 'I love you.'

'Perhaps you do.' His eyes weren't searching, but still on her face.

Roslynn saw Sholto first at his rooms, and the following afternoon Dr Grosvenor.

'You can get dressed now, young lady,' the big man said briskly. 'Nothing wrong with you. A clean bill of health.'

'Thank you, Doctor.' Roslynn brought herself up into a sitting position and Sister came towards her.

'Let me help you, my dear.'

Thank God for that, she thought, when briefly she had feared Dr Grosvenor might have found something unexpected. No two men could have been more different than Sholto and the big, burly Dr Grosvenor. The doctor was rather a jolly man, his twinkling blue eyes revealing his thoughts, whereas yesterday Sholto had definitely overawed her, more distinctly the brilliant surgeon, so that Sholto, the man, briefly ceased to exist.

'Now, sit down right there,' Dr Grosvenor told her reassuringly when she went back into the other room to join him. 'You looked scared, my dear.'

'I suppose all patients have little fears.'

'Yes,' he agreed quietly. 'Don't forget doctors in turn are patients themselves. Not always good ones either.' His blue eyes crinkled with laughter and the remembrance of his own stay in hospital when finally Matron had to take him to task. 'Apart from the fact that your weight isn't really what it should be— you're a good eight to ten pounds down even for a small frame—your general health is good. I'll have a full report for Mr McNaughton. That was a beautiful job he did on you. Nothing less than superb.' The admiration was genuine.

Sister came with her to the door and Roslynn smiled and thanked the woman, deciding not to do any shopping but go straight on to the house. The McNaughton town residence, though not as large as their summer retreat, was far more imposing, built in the mid-1880's by Douglas McNaughton, an ambitious young Scotsman, a second son, though generously provided for by his father. A personal fortune had enabled him to start out on his adventures, but he brought more to his adopted country than gold. By the time he died, forty years later, the father of four notable sons, he was honoured and respected by the whole community;

a tradition the McNaughton men had apparently kept up.

Roslynn wandered along the gallery examining the family portraits at her leisure. The men were all stern-faced and handsome, the women simply looked patient and silent, waiting in the background. Until Elizabeth. Why, she was a beauty, an extremely vivid woman, fine dark eyes, a lovely mouth, a disciplined face well enough, but a face full of purpose and character. Her own woman. Sholto had told her the portrait had been completed when Elizabeth was in her thirtieth year, a woman doctor in a man's world. She would have had her problems forcing them to take her seriously. No matter how good a woman was, she had to fight for attention. At least she had convinced her husband.

Roslynn swung about to face the opposite wall. Sir Andrew McNaughton. It was a different portrait from the one that hung above the mantelpiece at the summer residence. He was older here, in his late fifties, but, Roslynn decided, just as handsome. Faces like that didn't grow old, the bones beneath were built for survival. Sholto was more like his grandfather than the father who had died so prematurely. Killed by overwork, Elizabeth had said. It must have broken her heart. For some reason neither of them spoke about Sholto's mother other than to mention that she had eventually remarried and now lived in Canada. There was no portrait of her either, and none of Sholto, but a magnificent painting of his sisters as teenage girls. The background was a dull green out of which canvas the young faces glowed.

They were all dark, like Sholto, but not with his exotic eyes. The girl who was seated, Sarah, would have been about twelve, the older girls, Catherine and Fiona, one leaning, one standing, a few years removed. They were all extremely good-looking, Sarah with a look of Elizabeth, Catherine and Fiona set apart.

Even as she looked at them she was brushed with mourning. There were no reminders of her own sister Marianne, beyond a few photographs. She and Marianne had been physically unalike, but they couldn't have been closer. Marianne had been like a mother to her really, always ready to protect and defend her. In their childhood games when Kip had started to get boisterous, Marianne had always told him to stop. Jostling girls wasn't gentlemanly, she had admonished him as if she were ten years older. That was the curious thing; Kip had never really liked Marianne when he had always loved her. Since they had returned to England Roslynn had received several letters from Kip and Aunt Vanessa, even Jeremy had scrawled a few lines, but so far she had not replied to them beyond a brief acknowledgement. What was there to say?

Sholto came home very late, but still Roslynn waited up for him. Loving him so much had given her insight and she could see beyond his habitual controlled expression that some anxiety was gnawing away at him.

'You shouldn't have stayed up, Roslynn,' he told her quietly.

'I'm a night owl really.' And so she was. 'What's the matter?'

'Tired,' he said briefly.

'Have you had anything to eat?'

'I'm not hungry.' He shook off his jacket and placed it on a chair. 'Nick Grosvenor rang me. I guess we can celebrate.'

'Well, what would you like?' Roslynn paused, regarding him. 'Won't you at least tell me what's worrying you?'

Sholto looked faintly startled. 'Do I look worried?'

'Yes, behind the total detachment.'

'Then you're the only one to sense it.'

'Why don't we go into the kitchen and I'll fix you something to eat?' she suggested. 'I've always liked supper, ever since I've been a little girl.'

'And how you've grown!' It was the first lightness he had displayed. 'Maybe I will have something. I stayed to speak to one of my colleagues. We have a big operation lined up for Thursday morning.'

There was rebellion battling with the weariness. 'How old is the patient?' She took eggs out of the refrigerator to make him an omelette.

'Why do you ask that?'

She caught her lower lip pensively. 'Maybe I'm catching your struggle. The way you feel inside. I would say the patient is very young.'

'Five.' His long clever fingers found and fastened on the back of a chair.

'Oh,' she felt the pity well up inside her. 'That must hurt?'

'She was brought in after an epileptic fit—her first. The sweetest little girl you can imagine. A brain tumour.'

Her face and her voice were impassive because that was how it had to be. 'You *can* operate?'

'The tumour is in an operable position, but the whole thing is rather perilous. Her parents are distraught, the mother desperately refusing to believe it.'

'Why do things happen as they do?' Roslynn shook her head.

'Sometimes I think my job is like a battlefield.' Sholto sat down on the edge of the table, loosening his tie.

'Yes, it must be difficult to shut your mind.'

'But shut it I must. Emotion spells danger.'

'And you can't escape your destiny. You were born to be a doctor, the *best*.' She saw now how he might wish to keep himself apart, and her impotent love streamed out to him in a flood. She even felt remorse for goading him into admitting his desire for her. How could anyone enslave Sholto, or even try?

She gave a little sigh and began to beat the eggs vigorously, shunning her own femininity so he could look at her as if she were a houseboy. 'This won't take long.'

'Are you going to have any?' Looking at her revealing little face, he had to smile.

'No, I'm going to have toast. Mrs Harper made me an enormous dinner, but I still have a little room left.'

They sat down companionably, Sholto marvelling at her expertise with an omelette which she had flavoured with diced bacon and cheese and garnished with parsley from the home garden.

'I didn't think I wanted anything,' he said, and looked at her, 'but that was the very thing.'

'You look better already.' She turned his coffee towards him.

'You're going to spoil me, Roslynn,' he said.

'I'd rather spoil you than disturb you. One of the things I love in you is your dedication.'

'It can be. a tyranny,' he pointed out. 'My father worked himself into the grave. It was monstrous. The demands of his career smothered him.'

'Then you'd better try not to let the same thing happen to you. Look at it this way, you're no good to your patients if you kill yourself.'

'Maybe I need you to chat me up.' Sholto leaned back with his brilliant eyes half closed. Without make-up Roslynn looked younger than ever, her lovely mouth a natural rose-pink, her every thought mirrored in her eyes.

'You don't need me at all.' How brave to admit it.

'Oh, I think so, my little friend.' He caught her hand and held it. 'Maybe I should adopt you.'

'You're not going to worry about me at all.' Now she knew the absurdity of trying to force his love.

'No?' He said it with an intensity that shook her.

'In the New Year, I'm going off home.' She raised her head and looked into his sombre blue-green eyes. 'You said yourself I was caught up in a furious crush, but I'm going to resist it for your sake. I'm going to will myself elsewhere. I might even start a love affair with somebody else—Luke Edwards. He sat there the whole night staring at me.'

'Yes,' he said, taking a slow sip of the hot coffee, 'I

saw him. It's very good of you to sacrifice yourself in this way.'

'That sounded like mockery,' she said.

'It was.' A smile curved his beautifully delineated mouth. 'You're not going to concern yourself with Luke Edwards. He's a very lightweight young man.'

'True, but what else can I expect?'

'What you deserve,' Sholto said curtly.

It was no time for histrionics and she stopped herself from saying anything. She was going to rinse off the dishes and stack them away in the dishwasher and he was going off for a good night's rest.

'I can't think of anyone more beguiling than you when you're trying to be a good girl.' He sounded quite different now, warm and friendly.

'I genuinely *want* to be.'

His brilliant eyes narrowed over her face. 'Now hold on, little one, don't let anyone impose on you a different mould. You have to develop in your own way. You're a very spontaneous person. I don't want to see that stamped out.'

'I thought spontaneous people were demanding?' Roslynn said. 'It seems to me you don't want any demands on you at all. Certainly not from a woman.'

'It just seems that way to you.' He put his hand beneath her chin and tilted it so he could see her face. 'Maybe I only thought I could go it alone.'

The touch of his fingers on her skin was exquisite and she had to move. 'I take it you don't want any more coffee?'

'No, thank you.'

She could hear the smile in his voice, but it didn't

stop her from moving around energetically.

'I might take a Scotch up to bed, though.'

That sounded strangely like an amused irony. Roslynn struggled not to turn around, but she had to, only to find his eyes on her for an interminable time so that she was caught in a kind of demented longing.

'Why are you looking at me like that?' she asked.

'What do you think?'

'It sounded like you wanted to take me up as well.'

'That's what we're both afraid of.'

Unhurriedly he stood up, pushed in his chair and came towards her, moving with a deliberation that made her feel very small and lost.

'Sholto?' she said uncertainly.

'Goodnight, little one.' He drew her head towards him, upturned her mouth and barely brushed it with his own.

'Oh!' her little moan betrayed an ache.

'Don't feel so bad.'

His voice was so unbearably mocking that out of nowhere she wanted to hit him. 'You *beast*!' she exclaimed hotly. 'You're supposed to be a saint, but you're a devil as well.'

'A *saint*!' He threw back his head and brushed his hand across his eyes. 'Where in the hell did you get that insane notion?'

'Oh, around,' she said vaguely. 'It's never been *my* analysis.'

'God, I should hope not!' He smiled in genuine amusement at the thought. 'There's nothing remotely saintly about my feelings for you.'

'Nor mine for you.' She was whispering, almost.

'It almost seems as if some of the necessary ingredients for marriage are there,' Sholto pointed out blandly.

'I'm going to bed,' she said, stressing the fact that she knew he was teasing her.

'Good idea. Do you want me to carry you up?'

'I do not.' She looked back at him steadily and lifted her chin. 'Just don't think you're always going to be the great big adult.'

'In other words, Roslynn,' he returned seriously, 'you're going to let me take over your life?'

'If you want it, Sholto,' she said.

His eyes seemed to be raying through her, tremendously intense, as though his task was to discover every secret of her heart and mind. Then he reached out and grasped the whisky decanter. 'I suppose it was inevitable,' he said.

CHAPTER EIGHT

ROSLYNN went back to the mountain without Sholto because it was necessary for him to be on hand should the Price child need him. The operation had gone beautifully, but no one connected with it automatically assumed the worst was over. Just Sholto's presence alone had proved so reassuring to the young parents, their tremendous alarm had subsided and they really allowed themselves to hope.

'He must have been very worried,' Elizabeth said as they were sitting together discussing the events of the past week.

'I don't think I stopped praying,' Roslynn confided. 'Sholto said he sensed something was wrong even before he examined the child.'

'Yes, he's quite uncanny,' Elizabeth agreed with more than a touch of pride. 'A fantastic diagnostician.'

'I guess he told you all about it when he rang?'

'He did mention it only in passing. Sholto doesn't talk much about his work.'

'Did he talk about me?' Roslynn asked.

'*Reams!*' Elizabeth said more lightly, and laughed. 'You're probably his star patient.'

'Ex-patient.'

Elizabeth picked up the edge of tension in Roslynn's voice. 'You've got something to tell me, haven't you?'

'That's a beautiful portrait of you at the house,' Roslynn sidetracked.

'Don't get off the subject.' Elizabeth's fine dark eyes were searching, though her tone was definitely friendly.

'I don't think I know where to begin.'

'I suspect it happened at once,' Elizabeth said with a good deal of Sholto's dryness. 'You're going to tell me Sholto has decided to marry you.'

Roslynn, who had been sitting in an armchair jumped up. 'Have you got second sight?'

'I've been alive a long time.'

Roslynn sat down hastily. 'Oh, Elizabeth,' she said

urgently, 'tell me what I must do.'

'Do exactly as Sholto says.'

'But surely then you approve?' Roslynn's eyes filled with tears.

'Why, my dear child, it's a blessing!' Elizabeth insisted. 'I couldn't think of anyone I want more to join the family.'

That made the tears flow until Elizabeth had to stop her. 'Surely this is a joyous occasion?' she chided Roslynn affectionately.

'I'm sorry,' Roslynn dried her tears intensely. 'Do you know if he loves me?'

'Don't *you*?' Elizabeth asked in a startled voice.

'I think he feels more responsible for me than anything.'

'Stuff and nonsense!'

'No, listen, Elizabeth,' Roslynn laid her hand on the old lady's arm. '*I* did this.'

'You mean you twisted my grandson around your little finger?'

'He doesn't find it funny,' Roslynn insisted worriedly. 'We can't help knowing he's not an ordinary man.'

'Certainly not!'

'Whereas I *am* ordinary.'

'You're not.' Elizabeth was smiling, glad to answer her. 'You're a beautiful, intelligent, well-bred girl.'

'I haven't got enough to offer Sholto. The fact is, I'm too young. He calls me a baby.'

'The fact is,' Elizabeth corrected her, 'you need an older man and Sholto needs someone like you to cherish.'

Roslynn leaned over and gently kissed the old lady's cheek. 'You've been hoping Sholto would get married, haven't you?'

'I've been anxious,' Elizabeth admitted. 'He quite enjoys women really and they're certainly fond of him, but it's a lonely time being a doctor, a surgeon, no matter what Sholto thinks he does need a woman to love and care for him. I know Andy did, but he didn't want to know about it either. Really you can only help them by being there. Sholto *will* see that. He didn't have the rigid background my dear Andy did. Duty before everything. It was always sort of holy.'

'I expect *you* came as a surprise to the McNaughtons?' Roslynn asked more happily.

'I came as a surprise to Andy as well. Our courtship wasn't peaceful, and of course they had the girl picked out—an empty, egotistical creature with a fortune of her own. She hated me. In fact, she was insanely jealous. She caused a lot of trouble—but I'd rather not remind myself of those days. Our married life was magic and a sacrament. Real love is in very short supply.'

'Yes,' Roslynn agreed breathlessly.

'Well, there we are,' Elizabeth patted her hand. 'Family.'

'What will Laura think?'

'God knows!' Elizabeth responded in a low, emphatic tone. 'I expect, like Clarissa, she'll try to make trouble.'

'How?'

'The usual way, I should think,' Elizabeth

pondered, 'try to undermine your confidence. Stuff like you'd better understand at once that Sholto is merely sorry for you.'

A few days later when Roslynn was doing some shopping in the village, Laura was the very person she encountered.

'Why, Roslynn,' she called, her pale blue eyes lightening and widening. 'So you're back again?'

Roslynn felt like gulping, but instead she went forward smiling pleasantly. 'How are you, Mrs Edwards?'

'Oh, *Laura,* please. How stuffy you English are!'

Stuffy when we don't like someone, Roslynn thought.

Laura was staring down at her, frankly examining her from top to toe. Rather rudely, Roslynn thought.

'What do you say to a cup of coffee?' she asked at last. 'I've been shopping all morning and I have rather a head.'

Really before she had a chance to answer Laura began to hustle the girl towards the nearest open-air coffee shop, where perhaps a dozen people were enjoying watching the passing parade from the cool shelter of the gaily striped umbrellas and the lacy framework of the spaced trees.

'Ah, lovely!' smiled Laura when the young Italian waiter brought them coffee and a small plate of beautifully decorated cup cakes. 'Now we have a chance to talk!'

Roslynn gazed steadily into her cup and poured in a teaspoon of raw sugar.

'Sholto didn't come back with you?' Laura asked a little mournfully.

'No,' Roslynn shook her head. 'He wants to be on hand for any post-operative complications. He had a brain tumour on Thursday.'

'Dear God!' Laura shuddered. 'Sometimes I can't accept it at all, Sholto's being a neurosurgeon. It seems such a deadly branch of medicine.'

'Well, I can't accept that at all!' Roslynn sat more upright. 'Sholto saved me, and I guess a lot of people are very happy they came to him every hour of the day and night.'

'Oh, for heaven's sake, dear, you know what I mean,' said Laura, gently chiding. 'Surely many of his patients have no hope at all.'

'Well, if they don't, Sholto would be the last person to admit it. I don't think he'll be happy until he can save everyone.'

'Oh yes, he's a perfectionist I agree.'

'He's a great doctor.'

'And you, Roslynn,' Laura smiled at her very tightly, 'by the sound of it, you're in love with him. Roslynn didn't answer and Laura continued. 'It's not very intelligent, is it? Then again, just the sort of thing one might expect. Lonely, penniless young girl falls madly, deliriously in love with her doctor who just happens to be a very rich man.'

'Is he rich?' Roslynn asked.

'Of course,' Laura replied sharply. 'Inherited money and his own money as well. Sholto has always led a privileged life. I really don't think I have to tell you about it. There's their summer house and their town residence. Both properties would fetch a fortune.'

'I guess he's rich, then,' Roslynn said.

'Which doesn't mean to say little girls can just reach out and grab.'

'I beg your pardon?'

'Oh, don't come the lady of the manor with me, dear,' snapped Laura with scarcely veiled contempt. 'It distresses me in a way to have to say this, but it must be said all the same. I'm sure Elizabeth hasn't got the foggiest notion what you're up to, but *I* have. To put it plainly, leave Sholto alone. I'm sure you've spent the past week batting those soulful big eyes at him. They may even have affected him. As you so rightly maintain, Sholto is all heart. Why do you think he took you into his home? It distresses him to see suffering, but you're better now.'

'Yes, I am.' Roslynn couldn't even drink her coffee. 'Do you mind if I say I find you appallingly presumptuous?'

'Not at all.' Laura even laughed. 'But I do expect you to shut up about it.' There was a curious expression on her narrow face. 'I've spent most of my life loving Sholto, so I'm not going to allow any young girl to occupy room in his life. So he got you through a difficult time? Be grateful, my dear, but don't overwhelm him with your burning schoolgirl love. He doesn't want it, you know. In fact, knowing Sholto as I do, you must be causing him an unbelievable amount of embarrassment.'

'Does it matter much to you?' Roslynn asked quietly. 'Maybe you're lost in your own dreams.'

'What's that supposed to mean?' Laura asked so

violently that the woman at an adjoining table turned her head.

Roslynn looked steadily back at Laura's face. 'Sometimes we wish for things so badly we allow ourselves to believe our wishes might come true.'

'Oh, they'll come true all right,' Laura informed her sardonically. 'You see, I've fashioned myself to suit Sholto perfectly. It was different when we were younger, but I've learnt a lot. I've learnt not to want too much. One has to realise that with Sholto he can never neglect his work. The hysterical passions would only litter up his life. I lost him once because I couldn't accept a compromise, but I can promise him utter serenity now. He's come to see that. We've discussed marriage, of course. We even started planning, then along came little Miss Amnesia. I heard your touching story.'

Roslynn stood up unhurriedly and stood by her chair. 'Please excuse me, Mrs Edwards, I have to go. I'll pay my share at the counter.'

'Goodness me, no!' Laura gesticulated with her hands, 'it's my shout. You're not really much of a social mixer, are you?'

'It seems to me you have a few shortcomings yourself,' retorted Roslynn.

When she got back to the house Elizabeth was working in the garden, or rather Bill was working and Elizabeth was standing over him supervising. A new vista had been decided upon, defined by a recently arrived piece of statuary, and Elizabeth was dictating which garden beds should be laid out where.

'Back early, aren't you, Roslynn?' Elizabeth called. 'So much the better—you can tell us what you think.'

'What could be better than one woman's opinion,' said Bill, 'but two?'

There was no opportunity to speak then, but afterwards Roslynn confided bits and pieces of her conversation with Laura.

'Why, the cheek of her!' Elizabeth protested.

'Mind you, I wasn't all that pleasant,' Roslynn admitted.

'Well, well, well,' Elizabeth said. 'I didn't think she'd come out into the open so quickly.'

'I suppose she feels entitled to,' Roslynn pointed out rather desperately, 'she told me she and Sholto had discussed marriage plans.'

'Now, that was stupid,' Elizabeth said. 'I can't think of one important decision Sholto hasn't told me about. I don't believe that story at all.'

'She was adamant,' Roslynn said with a stirring of relief. 'She told me they'd even made plans.'

'No, dear,' Elizabeth answered quite rapidly, breaking off what she was doing. 'Sholto is the most honourable man I know. He simply wouldn't treat a woman like that.'

'It seemed extremely unlikely,' Roslynn seconded with her own conviction. 'How could he possibly tell me I was going to marry him and keep Laura on a string at the same time?'

'Well, it has been done,' Elizabeth pointed out with humour, 'but not by Sholto. I have the feeling we haven't heard the last of Laura.'

The first of the pre-Christmas parties started and invitations arrived by the score.

'Gosh, I've missed you,' Kris exclaimed, as he guided Roslynn through the groups of people, large and small, that congregated at his mother's party. Everyone seemed to have divided themselves off automatically; the fancy free, the young marrieds, the middle-aged and the comfortably retired, all of them relaxed and ready to enjoy themselves, glass in hand, munching on a lavish host of delicious hors d'oeuvres.

'A lot of people!' Roslynn observed.

'The whole mountain,' Kris stared around, seconding her statement. 'You'll see the same old faces wherever you go. We all go to each other's parties.'

So that meant Laura, Roslynn thought dismally, and surely enough she arrived with Luke and Luke's mother and father. The father was a short man but incontestably pleasant-looking, the mother rather better looking than most, but Laura looked superb.

'Merciful heavens!' Kris affected a falsetto voice. 'Here come the Edwards. Mind you, Joe's not a bad bloke.'

Already Laura was giving Roslynn a meaningful stare and a moment later Luke pounded over to them wearing a huge grin.

'Hale and hearty, I see!' His eyes travelled boldly over Roslynn in her lovely mauve crêpe dress, sashed around the tiny waist with silver. It had a very soft look, essentially romantic, whereas Laura's stunning outfit in a brilliant turquoise was easily the most dramatic there.

'Keep your eye off my girl,' Kris said without any attempt at gaiety.

'Isn't that a bit premature?' Luke's dark eyebrows rose.

'Oh, do let's enjoy ourselves,' Roslynn regarded them both levelly. 'I'm nobody's girl.'

'Actually I wonder. . . .' Luke murmured with what sounded like a spasm of malice.

Of course Laura had been talking, and Roslynn gave a delicate little shrug. 'Shall we go out on to the terrace?'

'Oh, please—I want you to meet my mother and father.' Luke grasped her arm.

Beside her Kris made a plaintive sound but Luke was bearing her off.

'Ah, our little visitor!' Laura exclaimed quite loudly. 'How are you, Roslynn? You look so . . . *pretty.*'

'Magical, I'd say,' Joseph Edwards supplied. Luke performed the introductions and Roslynn found herself barely acknowledged by Luke's mother, who nevertheless stared her up and down, affronted to meet the girl Laura had told her all about, but Joseph Edwards took her hand and looked into her eyes with a great big uncomplicated smile.

'So this is the young lady my son has been telling me about? I didn't think anyone could be so pretty, but as far as I'm concerned he was soft-pedalling it.'

Mrs Edwards glanced at her husband keenly, but he seemed oblivious of this frigid regard. Obviously he couldn't see any threat to the family, but Laura did, and so did Mrs Edwards on Laura's behalf. Both women were in fact leaning towards Roslynn in an unconsciously predatory manner as though they wanted to pick her lovely young face to pieces. It simply couldn't be allowed, it wasn't even remotely possible, that Sholto could be torn from their grasp by this penniless little newcomer barely twenty years old.

It was a very strange evening. Inevitably quite a few people indulged in a little gossip, and Roslynn was acutely aware of the heads turned her way and for the most part, kindly but speculative looks. For all her handsome countenance and general poise, no one really liked Laura, and they were only human in considering what this fascinating little English girl might do to her chances. Marrying Sholto off they had almost given up for lost, now this stranger in their midst brought a renewed interest.

'What the heck's going on tonight?' Kris mused.

'There's a story in it somewhere,' Roslynn returned flippantly. Kris was aware of all the glances given her, but he appeared to be unconscious of the thoughts and speculations behind the bright, quizzing eyes.

Luke joined them often, smilingly turning aside Kris's pointed comments. There was something insatiable about him as though he was convinced that persistence and determination would drive Roslynn into his fickle, sometimes cruel arms. Then too, he had seen the emerging situation at once, knew the dangers and had discussed them long and carefully with his late uncle's wife. Laura had in fact given him tremendous motivation towards gaining the little English girl's attention and trust—the promise of a new car, not any ordinary vehicle, but the excitement of a Porsche.

'What about having dinner with me one night this week?' he asked as Kris departed briefly to fetch Roslynn a plain mineral water.

'I'm sorry, Luke,' she smiled at him with an effort. 'Not possible.'

'Why not?'

'I could say we haven't a great deal in common.'

'And how would you know that?' he tapped his fingers against her delicate wrist. 'You won't even talk to me, much less look me in the eye. What are you afraid of?'

She eased her hand away unhurriedly. 'That's a curious word, Luke.'

'At the risk of sounding too sure of myself, I'd say you were.'

'Not at all.' Nevertheless some feeling of dread was jangling her nerves. 'In any case, Kris wouldn't like it at all.'

'But you're not interested in Kris, are you?'

'I like him a lot.' She stiffened at the barbed implication.

He merely shook his head, tossing his own drink down his throat. 'The fact is, sweetie, you've done the usual thing around here; taken a shine to the depressingly handsome and gifted, not to say formidable McNaughton. No, don't deny it,' he murmured as she turned her head aside, 'I know it probably started off as an all-powerful gratitude, then it grew into an equally powerful crush. You're only one of hundreds of females that haven't escaped it. Try as he undoubtedly does, Sholto can't help attracting women. For one thing, he's so damned terrific to look at, for another he's the great healer. So romantic!'

'You don't like him?' Roslynn asked.

'On the contrary,' Luke informed her, 'we're all hoping he's going to become part of our family. My Aunt Laura has a tenacious grip on him that she refuses to let go, and more awesome, my mother has joined forces with her to capture the mountain's most triumphant prize.'

'Good God!' Roslynn said quietly.

'Don't be bitchy, darling. You know what women are like. Men only think they're the hunters, when women are the greatest predators the world has ever known.'

'Some women,' she said tiredly. 'Most of us are gentle creatures.'

'How naïve!' He was genuinely amused. 'There's nothing gentle about Laura. Not when she feels she's being threatened, and who can blame her? It should be said, the noble Sholto has promised marriage, so that's a commitment he can't walk out on. Not the honourable Sholto McNaughton.'

'I don't think we should be discussing Sholto's affairs,' Roslynn said coldly, 'nor your aunt's. I don't think either of them would thank you for airing their private discussions.'

Luke laughed for a full minute. 'You *are* a little innocent!' he remarked, giving Roslynn a shrewd look. 'Laura wouldn't mind if I used a tape recorder providing it helped her land Sholto. I suppose it's nasty in a way but you know what they say—all's fair in love and war.'

'What do you think of loyalty?' Roslynn asked, relieved beyond measure to see Kris returning.

'A very sterling quality.'

'Yes, it is.' Roslynn stood up quickly, nodding her head. 'My loyalty is to Sholto, so I know you'll appreciate that I don't want to gossip about him behind his back.'

Luke stood up just as quickly, staring down at her with a pleading, apologetic expression. 'Please don't be offended, Roslynn,' he said urgently. 'I'm really trying to help you. Laura is as jealous as hell, and I think you should know.'

Now Roslynn was angry, but she spoke very quietly. 'I can't see why, Luke, except maybe she's over-possessive. If Sholto has promised to marry her what more could she want?'

'For you to go away,' Luke sighed deeply, 'or else fall for somebody else. I think the way I fell for you the first time I saw you. To put it plainly, Kris isn't the only one who's nuts about you. Why don't you give me a chance?'

His gaze was full on her, unashamedly bold, taking in her hair and her face and the delicate thrust of her breasts against the mauve crêpe of her dress. She knew he wanted to touch her badly, but she couldn't even begin to meet his desire. Everything that was in her, all her vulnerable passions, were for Sholto. For good or bad. The thought upset her so much she

swung away, so that Kris had to lift her glass of
sparkling mineral water on high.

'Whoops!'

'I'm sorry.'

'Drink it down, pet,' he bade her. 'Supper's
ready.'

After that, despite Kris's disappointment, Roslynn
turned down several invitations that came her way.
She had not the slightest desire to encounter the
Edwards again, and it was almost certain she would
have had she attended the brunches, barbecues and
pool parties organised for the holiday season.
Christmas was almost upon them and still Sholto had
not arrived. His little patient, the five-year-old Price
child, had suffered an initial setback, but to everyone's profound relief and intense joy had rallied to
make a steady rate of recovery.

'At last we might see him,' said Elizabeth. 'I
couldn't bear Christmas without Sholto.'

So that each of us in our own separate way is
missing him unbearably, Roslynn thought. She had
come to love in the quickest, earliest way. She knew
exactly what she felt, trusted her own head and her
heart, now it only remained to Sholto to choose the
woman he wanted for his wife. Although two people
had told her quite seriously that Sholto had discussed
marriage plans with Laura, but he himself had told
her all he felt for Laura was the affection of a long
acquaintance. Whenever her heart and her hopes
plummeted she held on to that. Lies were told all the
time for any number of reasons; to tangle, to capture,

for jealousy or revenge. Roslynn knew she had Sholto's full measure. He would never propose marriage to one woman and shame another with his betrayal. It would be enormously cruel and therefore completely out of character. If Sholto's avowed intention had been to marry Laura, then Roslynn, from her knowledge of him, was certain he would have already done so. Still she was not satisfied he had not thought about it, and that made her cry. Laura was his friend, a special friend; she must not forget that.

The porch lights were on for her when she arrived home from dinner and a quiet evening with Kris and his parents.

'Come over for a swim tomorrow,' Kris invited, 'it's so hot.'

'I'd love to, Kris,' she told him lightly, 'but there are a few jobs I simply must do for Elizabeth.'

'Such as?' Kris caught her around the waist and swung her to him.

'Oh, do the flowers, finish off the tree. You probably haven't heard yet that Sholto's sister Sarah is flying in with her two children.'

'Really?' Kris sounded surprised. 'What day is that?'

'The twenty-ninth, I believe.'

'Oh, good! She can come to our New Year's party. I'm glad it's Sarah. She's the easiest of the lot. Cath and Fiona are rather stuffy, I'm afraid.'

'Are they?' Roslynn asked, sinking back against a white column.

'That's the trouble with a lot of women when they consider themselves important. You know, the tides of power. All Sholto's sisters married very well, but only Sarah remained much the same. The spark of Elizabeth in her, I suppose. Now Sholto, who really *is* exceptional, smiles sweetly at us all. When he remembers us, that is,' Kris added wryly. 'Any idea when he's coming home?'

'None, I'm afraid.'

'I expect he'll have to for Christmas,' Kris told her kindly. 'I heard that little sigh.'

'You sounded pretty sorrowful yourself,' Roslynn charged him.

'Sholto taught me how to ski, did you know that?'

'I'll bet he didn't teach you how to drive.'

'I'll punish you for that!' Kris roared. He made a mock lunge for her, but though she held up her slender arms defensively, her clear laughter broke out.

Unexpectedly Kris sobered, clasping her lightly within the circle of his locked arms. 'Aren't you the least bit interested in me, little Roslynn?'

'Of course I am!' she protested.

'No, seriously, I mean it.'

'How seriously, Kris?' Her luminous eyes touched his face.

'I really like you, you know that. It would be very easy for me to love you, given any encouragement at all.'

'Oh, no, Kris,' she sounded distressed. 'I want us to be friends.'

'That's not easy,' he said wryly, 'not with a girl like you. There's something so deeply feminine about you, sort of startlingly so. I know you're younger than I am and so forth, but a lot of the time you make me feel you know ten times more than I do as a human being. You fit in easily with all age groups. I've seen you talk to Mum and Dad and a lot of people I've thought far too weighty for me and then I think—what can she possibly see in me?'

'A good friend, I hope?' Roslynn put up her hand and placed it lightly along his cheek. 'Don't resent me because girls always mature quicker.'

'Not all girls,' said Kris. 'A lot of them have a capacity for frivolity even I lack. The thing is you're not frivolous at all and I have to approach you seriously because of it.'

Roslynn could feel his strong young arms trembling. She wanted to tell him it was useless to fall in love with her, tell him now, so that he could stamp it out, but Kris took her silence for some kind of encouragement or he couldn't hold out much longer.

'Oh, Roslynn,' he said groaningly, and sought her upturned mouth.

'Kris!' Her body was arching, not towards him but away but just as she thought he couldn't even have heard her, the front door opened and a man's tall outline was silhouetted against the brilliant radiance of the chandelier.

The two of them stayed on in their impassioned pose, Kris's breathing ragged. It was Sholto, holding a newspaper in his hand, and if Kris was vaguely dreading what might be said, Sholto's voice sounded quite normal in every respect.

'Hi, Kris, my friend.' He came down the stairs, holding out his hand.

'Glad to have you back, Sholto.' Kris cleared his throat. 'Roslynn and I were just saying it would be terrible if you didn't turn up for Christmas.'

'Actually I thought you were trying to kiss her for all you were worth.'

'Except I wasn't able to.' Kris blossomed under the mocking, but essentially friendly smile.

'Then you won't be able to now,' Sholto said. 'It's bedtime for Roslynn.'

'Surely that's for me to decide?' Roslynn tilted her chin a little recklessly.

'Of course,' agreed Sholto, 'and I'm going to let you. Say goodnight to Kris.'

'Goodnight, Kris.' Roslynn gave him her hand and Kris raised it gallantly to his mouth.

'I wish I had your way with women, Sholto,' he said.

'There's really nothing wrong with your own way,' Sholto told him. 'How are things at home?' He started to walk towards Kris's car and both young people followed him.

'Oh, fine!' Kris said happily. 'Mum will be overjoyed you'll be able to come to at least one of her parties. You will, won't you?'

'Oh, I expect so,' Sholto returned blandly. 'We'll see.'

'Okay. Good.' Kris opened the car door and looked at Roslynn for a moment. 'If you can fit in that swim, just let me know.'

'I don't think so, Kris. Not tomorrow.'

'Ah, well!' he shrugged heavily, 'I don't love you any the less for it.'

'Perhaps he would if you didn't allow him to kiss you,' Sholto observed dryly, as Kris stalled the little car half way down the drive, honked the horn cheerfully, rectified matters, then started off again.

'What's sauce for the goose is sauce for the gander. It amounts to the same thing.' Absurdly because she was melting inside she felt almost an obligation to fight with him.

'I'm pretty sure I don't know what that means.'

Roslynn shrugged her delicate bare shoulders. 'Think about it.'

'Which, what?' He gave a low laugh in his throat. 'Come back into the light. I want to look at you.'

'Did you miss me?' Roslynn asked.

'Don't sound so hot and bothered.' He reached out a long arm and pulled her gently towards him.

Her response she felt deeply, as he no doubt already knew, wielding as he did so much power. Sensations could be so exquisite they were pain, and because she was so unsure of herself she was slow to look at him. She saw only his tall outline, the pale glimmer of his shirt, sensed the angle of his dark profile as he stared down at her reflectively.

'Wasn't it possible to let us know you were coming?' she asked, still in the same cool little cut-glass tone.

'I'm sorry,' said Sholto,' you were out when I rang.'

'Never mind, you had plenty of time.'

'So how have I spoilt your happy mood?'

'You must have to make quite an effort to re-member me.' Roslynn knew she was being childish, but it was all the same; he thought of her as a child.

'Now what did I do to deserve this?' Sholto murmured to the several brilliant stars that broke through the treetops. 'Broke up a loving exchange? No one likes that.'

'Don't be silly,' Roslynn said uneasily.

'And you're so sensible, after all?' His vibrant voice was edged with sarcasm. Or she considered it to be sarcasm.

'Not even *you* are truly sensible,' she said stormily, when everything about her craved to go into his arms.

They were in the leafy darkness of one of the great shade trees that guarded the house and Roslynn was obliged to stop because Sholto suddenly stood in front of her and took her shoulders, his thumbs stroking the satin skin along her collarbones. 'Do you want me to make love to you?'

'Yes.' She had intended to deny it, or say nothing, but the heat he was generating made deception impossible. Her trembling had begun at their very first contact, so astonishingly intimate and exciting, the expression of his unique effect on her. As he covered her open mouth, her heart fluttered and she fell forward against him, the initial superb response almost robbing her of strength.

Her glowing head was thrown back across his arm, the long white throat arched in ecstasy, and if he had held himself in control it suddenly went spiralling away. The clever hands, the cool intellect, the long years of self-discipline were servant to the power of passion. Somehow they were sinking together on to a dry bed of leaves and he moved her small slender body against him so that it was torment in its most exquisite form.

'*Sholto!*'

'Yes?'

She was gasping with sensations, engulfed in them, but his voice was hard and hungry, totally different from her own.

'Do you even understand what you're wanting?' he asked her.

'I know I want you desperately.'

'And I you.' He had turned her in his arms so now she was lying half across him. 'It's like nothing I've ever known before.'

'Is that why you're afraid of me?' she whispered, sliding her hand through the loosened buttons of his shirt. His skin was velvet to her satin, the powerful rib cage finely matted with hair. She could hear his heart pounding, feel it beneath her exploring fingers, the unprecedented pleasure of just stroking his skin. It was the most sensuous, luxurious feeling.

'Witch,' he muttered with bitter-sweet irony. 'You could become the most important thing in my life.'

'I love you,' she said, and he sighed deeply and reversed their positions. His hands on her body were both gentle and masterful, dissolving her fears and her flesh. Her breasts were naked now, not cool and she turned her head from side to side as he caressed one and then the other with his mouth. Much as she loved him she was still not fully prepared for the eroticism. He was an experienced man and she knew almost nothing.

Her blood was singing, winging through her veins. She knew what she wanted; everything that was forbidden, her body frantic for his.

'You've never made love before, have you?' Sholto asked.

'I thought it was something,' she said shakily. 'Kip used to kiss me all the time.'

'Little girl!' He lifted his head and his eyes flashed.

'I'm sorry,' she said meekly, apologising for she wasn't sure what.

'Little fool.' His sparkling eyes focused on her mouth. 'What it is to be trusted completely!'

'You should stop me,' she said. 'You have only yourself to blame, Sholto. You could have stopped me at the very beginning when you knew I was helplessly in love with you. I swear I'm deeply ashamed, but it was like being in some terrible limbo. A lot of dreadful things happened to me and you were the one thing in my life that kept me going. Kept me living. I can only say I'm not surprised if I frightened you with what seemed like an hysterical crush. I hate it as much as you do, but everything's different now. I've grown up.'

'Does this mean you're going to go all independent on me?' he challenged.

'I think you'll agree it's better,' she sighed. 'Of course I love you and it *is* love, but I would never want to trap you with pity or your sense of responsibility or whatever. I don't want you like that.'

'A beautiful thought!' Sholto bent his head and kissed her mouth. 'All of which has absolutely nothing to do with the way I feel about you.'

'Believe it or not, I know!'

He laughed quietly at the tartness in her voice. 'Oh, and how's that?'

'If you're looking for a wife at all, she has to be young and ready to be made over.'

He took it calmly. 'Do you think so?'

'What if I want to share your life fully, not remain in the background? I don't think I'm a background person.'

'I'm sure you're not.' His voice was spiked with self-mockery. Very expertly he rearranged the tiny shirred and ruffled bodice of her strapless sun-dress. 'This is a very provocative garment.'

'It wasn't meant to be,' she said emotionally, 'just pretty and cool.'

He had her sitting up, pressing kisses along the side of her neck as though she were a sweetly scented, well beloved child who needed comforting somewhat, until she turned her head on a tide of yearning and he covered her mouth again in a kind of hopeless goading. It was the most natural yet the most dangerous thing in the world, so deeply seductive even he was caught in the perilous web of passion.

Ultimately this kissing, no matter how heart-stopping, could not be enough, so that it was with a great sense of shock that Roslynn felt his fingers in her short curls, grasping and holding her head back.

'This can't go on, Roslynn, for a number of reasons.'

'What *is* it that happens?' she asked him. 'Why *is* it I'm drawn so powerfully to you? You were never a stranger even before you'd spoken a word.'

'Kismet, karma, preordination—the lot!' Sholto was looking beyond beyond her as she leaned against his shoulder.

'You don't need to marry me,' she said, her voice a little sad. 'If I'd been stronger at the beginning I could have managed to hide what I felt for you, but I was so sick and so frightened and alone. I'm not now. I'm beginning to get my old sense of self back.'

'I can see that too,' he told her. 'Actually you're quite a character, very spontaneous and honest.'

'Then I'm going to be honest now.' Roslynn knelt up on her knees, put her two hands on his shoulders and tried to stare into his eyes. 'I wouldn't consider marrying you for one moment unless I was certain you loved me, and I've heard nothing about love so far. I know you feel a lot for me and more violently than I thought but it's not of necessity love.'

'What is it, then?' he probed.

'I'm not going to persuade you,' she said.

'I think you could, rather beautifully.'

'No, Sholto.' She stood up and held out her hand. Tiny leaves clung to her, crushed and aromatic. She thought she would collect them all and keep them for a lifetime.

Sholto took her outstretched hand but brought himself up easily. 'In any case, Miss Ferrier, we've got to pull all the parts of your young life together. There are decisions you have to make about your property in England, whether you feel any commitment to your family, whether you want a complete break away from me, from the urgencies of the situation. You're so young!'

'So I can't know my own heart?'

'You've had little time to know what life is all about,' he told her gravely. 'I'm thirty-five to your nineteen.'

'Twenty in February, and it's almost that now.'

He shrugged and his words emerged more clipped than usual. 'You must have complete freedom to know your own mind.'

'I suppose what you're really trying to say is, you want me to go. After all, you don't want any woman to get too close to you.'

'I'm not saying that at all,' Sholto said quietly. He bent down, cupped her downbent head and lifted it up to him. 'You could be mistaken in what you feel for me.'

'I'm not.'

'You've been too close to me to tell.'

'Tell me something,' she said. 'Have you ever made love to Laura? Promised to marry her?'

He didn't even hesitate, though it was obvious he was angry. 'Laura and I have known one another a long time. A lot of people would say we're old friends and I've tried to do a lot for her. Mostly because of Frey. *He* was my friend. I've never had an affair with Laura and I've never even thought about it. She doesn't attract me in that way—but while we're on the subject, I've had my share of them. At least two in Laura's circle.'

'It's a wonder she didn't claw their eyes out,' Roslynn interjected.

'Obviously she didn't know, and even if she did, no area of my life is any concern of Laura's.'

'Poor Laura!' Roslynn sighed. 'Surely you know she loves you?'

'It pleases Laura to love someone she can't get. I've known her since she was your age. I was the same to her then as I am now. She had a man who loved her, but her stupidity robbed him of his dignity and almost robbed me of a friend. Even so, I feel a degree of caring for her. She would do anything for me and has, in fact, done me many favours—favours I didn't want from her but couldn't really turn aside without hurting her. I have never, ever, mentioned the word marriage. I couldn't have Laura crowding me with her obsessions.'

'So what about me?' Roslynn was almost speaking to herself. Hadn't she too crowded him beyond his limit?

'I've made up my mind about you,' he said briefly. 'Let's go back into the house and speak of more ordinary matters.'

CHAPTER NINE

Aunt Vanessa saw her return to England as conclusive proof that life would continue as it had before, but even a month later Roslynn still kept her decisions secret. Her life at Lakeview, no matter how beautiful it was—and it was beautiful in its time-mellowed warmth and livibility—was over. The young men she had once known had all sought her out, continued to do so despite Kip's hovering presence, but there was no mistaking where her heart was; fourteen, fifteen, God knows how many thousand miles away. Real love, when it came, there was no mistaking. Once she had thought herself in love with Kip. She had been happy with him, they had been very much the same, or so she had thought. Tragic events, no matter if that love *had* been real, would forever stand between them. Besides, in those days she didn't know what love was all about. She knew now and it didn't make her happy, it was a savage, tearing pain.

Kenneth, watching her as she walked to and fro in the garden, knew things would never be the same, but still, like his mother, he clung to his hopes. He wanted Roslynn now, more than ever, but she had experienced something in her life that had changed her for ever. Not that he wanted to acknowledge it, but it was there behind her wide eyes.

When he came up to her she turned to him smilingly. 'This is one of my favourite views.'

'Keep smiling, Rosa,' he said. 'What are you really thinking these days?'

'I feel like walking some more. Come with me?' she said.

'I can't think of anything I want to do more.' He was startled for a moment that she had asked him. In all the past month she had never deliberately sought out his company.

'How's business?' Roslynn asked.

'Dad's happy.'

'No one is forcing you to work for him.'

'What else can I do?' Kenneth shrugged defeatedly. 'I was never a brain. I'm not at all ambitious, as Mother says frequently, puttering away in an antique shop suits me fine.'

Roslynn didn't answer. Jeremy was happy because he genuinely loved beautiful things. It had always surprised her that Kenneth had joined his father in the shop, but now she saw it as an excuse not to do anything else. Kenneth had always liked the easy way out.

'I saw you had mail from Australia,' Kenneth prompted.

'Yes, a letter from Lady McNaughton.'

'May I ask about anything important?'

'Not really,' Roslynn said evasively, grateful beyond belief for any news of Sholto.

'Well, I never liked them much,' said Kenneth. 'Formidable old ladies aren't my favourites, and *he* was an arrogant devil.'

'You sound as though you envied him?'

'Sure you're not cold?' Kenneth turned to her as they climbed the hilly rise. 'I notice you've been rugged up a bit since you got home.'

'Don't forget I came from high summer.' There were lots of ways of being cold, Roslynn thought.

'You liked Australia, didn't you?'

'I loved it.' Roslynn said it more passionately than she intended and Kenneth lost his smile.

'You didn't fall in love with that McNaughton fellow, did you?'

'Yes.'

'You'll get over it.'

'*Never!*'

'You never felt that way about me,' he said with a kind of weary acceptance. 'What did I do wrong?'

'I don't think it's ever a question of right or wrong, Kip,' she answered him. 'It just happens. Often against what one really wishes. Whatever it is, it means the old life is over. The way you were, just like that!' She threw her hand into the air. 'For always. I fell in love with Sholto as soon as I opened my eyes after the accident. His were, and are, the most remarkable eyes I've ever seen. They kept me alive. He kept me alive. I only had Sholto at that time. Now I have my pride.'

'You mean he doesn't love you?'

'His work is very important in his life,' Roslynn said evasively.

'Poor little Rosa!' he said with deep, unchangeable affection.

She was reminded of the time when life had been carefree. Maybe all the way back to sixteen. Things had started to become complicated not all that long after that. Kip had begun to see her in more than a cousinly light and Marianne had always tried to put distance between them.

'What really happened that day on the lake?' she asked him.

'Are we never going to leave that alone?' Finally he turned to look at her, hazel eyes empty of anger, evasion.

'I can't, Kip. You know that. Just talk to me. Tell

me the way it was and I'll listen. I'm past hysteria and accusing.'

'But still you'll hate me. To know you'll never forgive me is quite enough.'

'So it's true.' She felt chilled and slightly light headed.

'Not as vile as that!' Kenneth moaned. 'God, Rosa, you couldn't possibly think me a murderer?'

'No,' she said hoarsely, and reached out and seized his arm. 'But I must know.'

'I only hesitated,' Kenneth began, his voice just above a whisper. 'Just a moment of hesitation, love. Marianne never called help and I thought she'd only faltered for a moment. Just for a few instants I couldn't make myself go to her. She'd been complaining of me all the time, doing everything she could to turn you against me when I cared for you more than anyone else in the world.' The tears were now running down Kenneth's cheeks, but he didn't notice them. 'I could never have saved her, Roslynn, even if I had moved immediately. She had a weak heart. It just gave up.'

'Dear God!' A dark haze was moving before Roslynn's eyes.

'At first the feeling of fear and guilt nearly crushed me,' Kenneth continued, 'but Mother forced me to open up. I told her how it was, exactly as I'm telling you, and she became just as violently upset, but she understood, Rosa. I never truly realised Marianne was in extremity. We've been swimming in the lake since we were children. I just thought a good shake-up would serve her right. The instant she disappeared of course I moved. You were there. You know I risked my own life.'

It was an endless moment, one that could spin out for as long as they both had life.

'So that's the way it was,' Roslynn said steadily.

'I love you,' Kenneth said, 'and I know I've lost you. It was what Marianne wanted, after all.'

A few days later Roslynn had a long meeting with Hugh Turner, the family solicitor.

'You can't be serious, Roslynn,' he said, looking across the desk at her closely as though searching out any signs of mental illness.

'Very much so,' Roslynn glanced down at her locked hands. 'I want Aunt Vanessa to have the use of the house during her lifetime and after that, if *I* am still alive, I'll decide what's to happen to it. I intend to go back to Australia. It's a new country, a new life. I got to love it.'

'But so far away!' Hugh sighed as if he saw some awful, Colonial existence.

'Marianne's share of the money I want to go towards medical research. I've got a list here.'

'May I see it?' Hugh extended his hand. 'Ah, very worthy, but it's an awful lot of money and it's yours now, not poor little Marianne's.'

'That's what I want, Hugh,' Roslynn said with quiet conviction. 'I have more than enough and the royalties are still coming in from my father's books.'

'Such a life you've had!' Hugh said, thinking of that wonderful man, his beautiful wife and that sober little creature Marianne who had so despised Vanessa who had looked after them for years. At least Roslynn knew something about gratitude, but then she had always been a tender-hearted little thing. Hugh sighed again.

When later in the day Roslynn told Vanessa what she had finally decided, Vanessa went pale.

'No, I can't accept it,' Vanessa cried out emotionally. 'Haven't we had enough unhappiness? Where could we *go*?'

'I'm not asking you to go anywhere, Aunt Vanessa,' Roslynn explained quietly. 'The house is yours for your lifetime. I care too much about you to turn you out. I know you love Lakeview as much as I do. *Did*,' she corrected herself without haste.

'But my dearest girl,' Vanessa, though she had regained a little of her colour, still looked distressed, 'we couldn't possibly maintain a house like this. It's been *your* money all along that has done that.'

'And it will still be there for that purpose.' Roslynn paused while she thought about the strange set of circumstances that had all but forced her from her home; the house that her father had loved and was always 'jolly pleased to get back to' no matter the exotic, far-flung places he travelled to.

'Oh, my dear,' Vanessa sighed, staring at the girl's saddened but somehow strengthened young face, 'can't we work this all out, whatever it is?'

'I have worked it out, Aunt Vanessa,' Roslynn pointed out gently. 'I've been a child too long. It's about time I looked after myself. I'm going back to school—university. Father would have wanted that, and I'm going to write. Whatever is in me

I'm going to see if I can shape it into a novel.'

'I'm sure you could,' Vanessa said quite seriously. 'How could it be otherwise? You've got a good deal of Charles in you. Jeremy only reminded me of it the other day. Write a book by all means, I can see you might like to, but can't you do it here?'

'No.' Roslynn looked out of the window reflectively, and Vanessa thought yet again how her youthful beauty had been strengthened and refined. Roslynn had always been a very pretty girl, but now her face had taken on a new cast as though suffering had made her very quickly a woman.

'All right, then,' Vanessa sighed. 'I hope before you go away, Roslynn, you'll find it in your heart to forgive Kenneth for whatever it is you're holding against him.'

'We've spoken,' Roslynn said briefly.

'Then you'll know he can take no more. It's a terrible thing to feel crushed by guilt, to be reminded of it again and again when really the whole feeling is irrational.'

'Not entirely irrational, Aunt Vanessa.'

'What did he say, then?' Vanessa flushed violently.

'He told me the truth.' Roslynn looked down at her joined hands. 'He only hesitated for a moment— oh, I understand! I remember how perfectly horrible Marianne was to him on occasions——'

'Well, that's *something*!' Vanessa snapped, unable to control a shudder. 'I often wanted to take Marianne to task, but I never did. She always had the whip hand. She was the elder and you two girls owned the house. Really, in a lot of ways and but for you, it would have become an intolerable position.'

'Only Marianne died.' Roslynn experienced again the same old feeling of helpless grief, all the familiar love for her sister. 'Poor Marianne, so strong, yet so frail.'

'She was trying to run your life.'

'She was trying to protect it,' Roslynn said in a calm, controlled voice. 'Can't you see now, Aunt Vanessa, that Kip and I aren't really suited?'

'No, I can't see that at all.' Vanessa was back into playing the part of an ambitious mother. 'You've got everything in common, but you're still allowing the ghost of Marianne to ruin your life.'

'No.' Just for a second Roslynn's nerves were terribly on edge, but she fought and won the battle for composure. 'I'm my own person now.'

'That's good, dear.' Because she was genuinely very fond of the girl, Vanessa spoke more gently. 'One can hardly suppose all your sufferings haven't had their effect on you. All I'm saying is, if you give yourself time, everything will work out.'

'I know that, and I'm going back to Australia.'

'But that's totally crazy!' Vanessa protested, looking wretched. 'Surely you haven't gone and fallen in love with that McNaughton man?'

'How could I not?' Roslynn said ironically.

Vanessa jumped up, went to the window and stared out in a dazed way. 'You have to see the predictability of all this,' she said forcefully. 'He's a very handsome man and I'm afraid he became almost godlike in your eyes.'

'He did for a bit,' Roslynn smiled. 'But he's very much a man.'

'Now what does that mean?' Vanessa swept around on her. 'Tell me, I want to know.' Her hazel eyes had an accusing glint.

'He suggested we should get married.'

'Well, really!' Vanessa gave an almost hysterical laugh. 'He's years older than you are.'

'Thirty-five to my twenty.'

'Quite unsuitable!' Vanessa insisted.

'I don't think I could have fallen in love with a better man if I had the whole world to choose from. He's perfect for me.'

'Oh, dear!' Vanessa sat down again quickly. 'And how did this happen?'

'Love at first sight for me,' said Roslynn.

'My dear, there's no such thing,' Vanessa looked at her pityingly.

'For most people, maybe,' Roslynn gave the older woman a reassuring smile, 'but for some of us, it happens. It happened to me and I'll never change my mind. I love Sholto and I'll always love him whether I marry him or not.'

'But if you aren't going to marry him, what are you going back to Australia for?' Vanessa asked fretfully. 'Really, Roslynn, I can't believe in this at all.'

'I'm sure you will,' Roslynn said in answer. 'I know my feelings for Sholto, but I don't know his exact feelings for me.'

'Probably fun while it lasted,' Vanessa said cruelly. 'After all, you're a beautiful girl and doubtless he realises you're extremely well off.'

'I can't think he considered that,' Roslynn murmured, scarcely affected by Vanessa's words. 'Sholto's not interested in money.'

'Darling, *everyone* is interested in money,' Vanessa pointed out slightly hysterically. 'I've never heard of anyone turning it down.'

'There's no emphasis on money, Aunt Vanessa,' Roslynn said with certainty. 'I'm not so sure if I can compete with his profession.'

'Now *that* has the sound of sense to it,' Vanessa commented. 'You could become a very lonely woman.'

'Well, if Sholto really loves me, I'll have to think up lots of things to occupy my time. Like a family, for a start. I would love children.'

'I can't see that either,' said Vanessa. 'You're still a child yourself.'

Roslynn shook her head and the curls on her beautiful glowing head danced. 'If I've proved one thing to myself it's that I've finally grown up. I've lost my heart, I may even break it, but I'll still find a way.'

'You will too, I think,' Vanessa conceded, looking at her. 'This isn't the end of us as family, though?'

'No.' Roslynn reached out and grasped the older woman's hand generously. 'We came together long ago and together we'll remain.'

She returned to Australia quietly less than a fortnight later where the Southern Hemisphere was brilliant with autumnal colour and the city was still golden with the last of the summer's heat.

She tried to recall afterwards the feeling she had

when the jumbo touched down, but so many emotions were whirling in her it was difficult to isolate the dominant one until afterwards—homecoming.

On the long, wearisome flight and at the airport she allowed herself to fall into conversation with this one and that, but she only had one face in her mind. She thought she was starved for the sight of it. *Sholto.* It was absurd, of course. He didn't even know she was coming, though they had exchanged several letters. Letters, she cherished, warm and friendly, supportive, with no hint of passion from either side. Probably he was waiting for her to fall *out* of love with him, but that could never happen. That would be like relinquishing the most beautiful part of her life.

She came through the Customs and a porter raced towards her.

'I'll take your luggage, miss,' he smiled, and Roslynn nodded.

'Thank you. I was hoping I'd find a Sir Galahad.'

'No one to meet you, miss?' The man picked up her bags cheerfully and deposited them on the trolley.

'Not today.'

'English, aren't you?' He smiled at her with satisfaction. 'My old mum was born in England. London. We've sent her back a dozen times to see all the family, but now she reckons Australia's her home.'

'Probably she couldn't part with all this beautiful sunshine.' Roslynn walked after the little man, but as they emerged into the waiting area, a tall man separ-

ated himself from the crowd, came vividly, purpose-
fully, towards her, and of all things, Roslynn burst
into tears.

'Not being met, hey?' the little porter said happily.
'Not much!'

'*Roslynn!*'

She felt as though she was disintegrating entirely,
but he had her in his arms, his chin against her
downbent head.

'Shall I take the bags out to your car, sir?' The
porter had no intention of going away. He loved
joyful meetings, it made him feel good.

'Fine, thank you.' Sholto still kept his arm around
Roslynn and directed her to an exit.

She tried to wipe the tears away, looked up at him
and he smiled.

'Welcome home.'

It wasn't until they were driving away that she
asked: 'How ever did you know I was booked on this
flight?'

'I got it out of Gran,' he told her with an ironic
smile. 'When you're rested after your long trip I
might slap you. Kiss you. Maybe both.'

'I guess you're not going to kiss me now?'

'Not on the freeway.'

'All right, so where are you taking me? I'm booked
into the Wentworth.'

'You *were*,' he gave her a brief glance. 'Right now,
I'm taking you home.'

'So why aren't you at your rooms?'

'I have a colleague who can handle things.'

'Hah!' Roslynn retorted.

'So what does that mean?' He braked as they approached a red light.

She just looked at him and said nothing, feeling her love for him melting her very bones.

'You look beautiful,' he said. 'More beautiful.'

The tone and the intonation turned her heart in her breast. 'So do you,' she said shakily, neither of them saying whether they missed the other or not.

They were moving again, very smoothly, and Sholto began to ask her what she had been doing since last he had heard from her.

'Aunt Vanessa was rather worried you could be after my money,' she told him.

'I absolutely refuse to believe that,' he said.

She only laughed. 'Money has always been in her mind, probably because she never really had any. It's a little sad when one is insatiable for position. Aunt Vanessa loves being mistress of Lakeview and she handles the part very well. I could never turn her out. I owe her too much.'

'And Kenneth?'

'I don't know clearly what's going to happen to Kip. Maybe some strong young woman will come along and save him or make him think seriously about what he is and what he wants to be. *I* couldn't do it any more than I could erase the past. We parted as best we could, the affection we couldn't change, sorrow for what changed us. There wasn't any easier way to do it. It's hard when one tries to be honest with oneself and other people.'

'Well, what now?' Sholto put out his left hand and touched her cheek lightly, and so sensitive was her skin to him that he must have felt the tremble run right through her.

'I'm going back to study,' she said. 'Had my parents been alive it would have been expected, but somehow with Aunt Vanessa and Kip my life was being directed into other channels. Then too, I want to find out if I can write.'

'You can certainly write a letter,' he turned his head and smiled at her. 'Compulsively readable, even if I didn't rate a love letter.'

'And I didn't *get* one.'

'So there we are, unable to really communicate.'

The tone was more mocking than sombre and she looked at him quickly, but he was concentrating on the heavy traffic. Roslynn turned her face away and looked out of the window, tired from the long flight, rather lightheaded but full of an excitement that could not be denied.

'*I'm taking you home.*'

She closed her eyes.

When she opened them again, they were parked inside the garage and Sholto was leaning towards her.

'Wake up, little one,' he said.

'Oh,' she groaned lightly, 'I'm not much good at long flights. It's really better to arrive at night.'

'Once I've got you upstairs you can sleep as long as you like, though it's better to have a meal first and walk around for a bit to adjust the inner clock.'

'Yes, Doctor,' she smiled faintly.

'If you're sure that's what you want.'

Her head flew to stare at him, but he was out of

the car, coming around to the passenger side.

'Want me to carry you?' he asked.

'There's nothing the matter with me except shaky legs.' Roslynn slid out to stand up, but that brought her right into his arms.

'Sholto,' she turned up her face to him, defeated by her love, but he was moving her against him first, hands charged with energy so that electricity crackled along her veins.

'You are quite beautiful,' he said, 'and I've missed you unbearably.'

There was something different about his face, his eyes, his expression, as though he too was vulnerable, so intent on her he might have stopped breathing.

Her arms went around him and she pressed closer, but then he grasped her head again, turning her face back up to him. 'Come here to me,' he commanded, and as her mouth parted, enclosed it with his own.

There was nothing else, *nothing*, and he kissed her over and over, his desire increasing, never satisfied. Roslynn knew she was swaying, would have fallen, only he held her up to him, his mouth so questing the sensations were enormous.

I love you! Mind, body, spirit cried out. He was even hurting her, but she didn't care, luxuriating in this hard possession. Then, as though he realised he had caught her up a fragile flower, he forced himself to release her, saying her name softly.

'Does that mean you love me?' she asked him, studying those brilliant eyes.

'With every breath I take.' He was still half supporting her, although she was leaning back against the car. 'I think that's all too plain.'

'And you're used to hiding your emotions?'

He laughed and tucked her into the crook of his arm. 'Let's go up into the house. Mrs Harper won't be there. I sent her off to her daughter's.'

'But she's in New Zealand!' Roslynn protested, looking up at him swiftly.

'That's right.' Sholto narrowed his eyes at her. 'Any objections?'

'Well, there's no one to stop us making violent love.'

'I promise I won't unless you want me to.'

'Sholto. . . .'

He looked down at her, recognised all her feelings and picked her up. 'I think I wanted you to get over me.'

'Did you?' She looked into his eyes, unimpressed.

'*God!*' he muttered.

Inside the house flowers turned their faces to her, enormously welcoming. Everything was exactly how it was before, beautiful, mellow, well loved and well lived-in.

'I can't carry you any longer,' said Sholto, making a joke of his fluid strength. 'That's more like it!' They sank together into one of the deep sofas upholstered in a chinoiserie chintz. 'Now that we're so comfortable, you can go to sleep.'

'Yes,' she said dreamily, 'with you.'

'Please, darling, I care so much about you.'

'It's what I want.'

'God knows it's what I want too,' he said thickly,

'but I want something more for you. I want our wedding day to be the happiest day of your life, perfect, new, an inspiration.'

'Are you certain you're going to marry me?' she asked.

'More to the point, are *you* certain?'

'I came back,' Roslynn pointed out.

'And I gave up the struggle long ago. There's nothing I want more in my life than to have you with me for ever.'

'You can kiss me, can't you?' she said.

Sholto looked down at her and brushed his fingers through her hair, grasping the silky curls. 'I don't begrudge you a few kisses,' he smiled, 'devastating as they might be. I think I'd better take you up to Gran tonight.'

'Do you doubt your own control?' Her silvery eyes teased him.

'I do,' he said dryly. 'My body is crying out for you.'

'And what about your mind?' She tried to encircle his wrist.

'It followed you over to England, I think. I can't have the anxiety hanging over me. I need you at my side.'

'Oh, yes,' she said, as though she had suddenly thought of something, 'is it really true Laura got married?'

'To a very prosperous fellow not in his first youth.'

'Elizabeth said about sixty.'

'But very rich.' He leant his head back and sighed. 'Why the devil are we talking about Laura? Didn't she try to cause enough trouble? And that wretched young nephew of hers!'

'Well, I think you settled him, to be sure.' Now, many long weeks later, Roslynn could smile. Laura's plans and the way Luke had conspired to help her were long ago. It was even difficult to believe Luke had arranged a seduction scene that had left her walking miles up a winding road until Sholto had found her. The very next day the Edwards cut short their holiday on the mountain and Laura found herself at the end of a dream.

'Still sleepy?' Sholto asked in his beautiful, tender voice.

'Fine now.' She stretched her slender arms up and encircled his neck. 'Is it imperative we wait until we're married?'

'Yes, my precious one. You don't know me half so well as you think.' He moved her mouth to beneath his and kissed it slowly, his hands dropping to her breasts for a moment.

'Sholto,' she took a deep breath when he released her, her voice hushed with the realisation there were many mysteries to be revealed, 'I'm not certain if I'll be woman enough for you.'

'*Magic!*' his lips were at her ear, his arms tightly around her. 'For me, you're quite flawless.'

'Still, we can't stay the night?'

'No.' He tapped her on the chin and glanced down at his watch. 'You know as well as I do that would be extremely dangerous. Whatever my strong urges, I'm going to back off. You are my only, perfect love and I know what I'm talking about. I'll remind you on our wedding night—which will be as soon as I can arrange it.'

'Wonderful!' She lifted his strong, lean hand and kissed the palm. 'I like a man who can think positively.'

'Even when it makes me ache.' His blue-green eyes were like living jewels. 'I think I'll get you something to eat, but before that, we'll ring Gran.' He stood up unexpectedly, lifting her at the same time as though she were no more than a doll.

'Do you really think you're going to surprise her?' Roslynn asked, experiencing such a rush of happiness it was almost like floating.

Sholto stopped beside the phone, lowered her to her feet but kept his arm around her. He dialled the number slowly, because Roslynn was pressing little longing kisses along his jawline, but finally he heard his grandmother's rich, penetrating tone over the wires.

'Hi,' he said, his voice warm with love. 'Yes, she arrived over an hour ago. Yes, she's with me. . . .' He felt more than saw Roslynn's hand come up to take the phone. 'We've got something to tell you.'

'Hello, Gran,' Roslynn heard herself saying, her luminous eyes filled with tears. Gran. Sholto. *Home*.

A KNIGHT IN SHINING ARMOR

When Roslynn arrives in Australia after a long and exhausting flight, it is a cheerful and obliging porter who comes to her rescue as she struggles with her baggage. Little wonder she calls him "Sir Galahad."

In legendary Camelot, Galahad was considered the most chaste and selfless of all King Arthur's knights. One day, as the knights were sitting at the Round Table, the windows and doors of the castle mysteriously slammed shut, and into the room strode a tall and handsome young man wearing shining white armor. He introduced himself as Galahad—Sir Lancelot's long-lost son! So quickly did Galahad prove his virtue and bravery by a series of miraculous feats that he became the foremost knight in King Arthur's court.

There are many stories of the knights of the Round Table, but the one that most concerns Sir Galahad is the quest for the Holy Grail, the silver chalice from which Christ drank at the Last Supper.

One day, a vision of the Holy Grail appeared to the knights, and they vowed that each would spend a year and a day searching for it. The story of their travels and adventures makes up much of the Arthurian legends, but in the end only Sir Galahad was pure hearted and virtuous enough to find the Grail and gaze into it.

No one knows if King Arthur and the knights of the Round Table really existed. But that doesn't stop people from giving the name of Sir Galahad to any "knight in shining armor" who selflessly assists someone in need!